WRC
MCC
17800 Rd 20
FT MORGAN, CO
80701
DIANA & PERSIS
303 867 3081

LOUISA MAY ALCOTT

DIANA & PERSIS

Edited by
SARAH ELBERT

ARNO PRESS
A New York Times Company
New York—1978

First publication 1978 by Arno Press Inc.

Copyright © 1978 by Sarah Elbert

Diana and Persis has been published by permission of the Houghton Library, Harvard University and Mrs. F. Wolsey Pratt.

The Harriet Hosmer sculpture "Puck" appears courtesy of the National Collection of Fine Arts, Smithsonian Institution.

Library of Congress Cataloging in Publication Data
Alcott, Louisa May, 1832-1888.
　　Diana and Persis.

　　Bibliography: p.
　　I.　Title.
PZ3.A355Di　1977　[PS1017]　813'.4　77-11663
ISBN 0-405-10521-5

Manufactured in the United States of America

Acknowledgments

A number of people in Boston, New York and Ithaca encouraged and assisted the preparation of Louisa May Alcott's "art story" for publication. Mrs. William Kussin first listened to my description of current readers' interest in Louisa May Alcott in her wonderful Concord toyshop. She gave my subsequent letter to her sister-in-law, Mrs. F. Wolsey Pratt, who kindly wished me success and gave me her permission to use the manuscript of the art story.

The Louisa May Alcott Association, its director and staff at Orchard House generously showed me some of May Alcott's work and helped me to contact Jeanne Stump of the University of Kansas, whose diligent work on nineteenth century women artists supported and confirmed my hunch that the characters and art works in the manuscript were drawn from the vibrant circles of the "white marmorean flock."

Mr. William Bond and Ms. Carolyn Jakeman of Houghton Library, Harvard University kindly went through all the scholarly and technical steps necessary from the first quotes in my doctoral dissertation to consideration of a facsimile reproduction and finally gave permission for this publication on behalf of Houghton Library, Harvard University.

Mr. Edward Reno of Microfilming Corporation of America traveled to Cambridge and Concord, believed in the importance of the manuscript and finally introduced me to the editorial staff of Arno Press. Leslie Parr of Arno has been an extraordinarily sensitive editor and friend throughout the adventure of Diana and Persis.

I and all my sister historians working on nineteenth century women and American culture are deeply indebted to the works and the model of scholarly excellence set by Madeleine Stern. Her biography of Louisa May Alcott and her uncovering and publication of much that has been "hidden from history" are only a part of her rich contribution to feminist studies. Mary Beth Norton of Cornell University has kept the faith from the first days of my graduate research on Alcott as have Michael Colacurcio, Jonathan Bishop, Allison Lurie, Gould and Cynthia Colman. The Cornell Archives staff have always made me aware of the importance of archives in restoring our heritage.

The faculty, students and staff of the History Department at the State University of New York, Binghamtom, and the Women's Studies Program at Cornell provided intellectual stimulation and a rare degree of academic freedom. Their steadfast support of women's history remains the essential base upon which *Diana and Persis* and all of my work in cultural history rests.

Finally, Sander Kelman, Adam Kartman, and Carrie Kartman treated the manuscript and its editor with love and respect.

INTRODUCTION

Louisa May Alcott's sister May recorded in her diary on January 28th, 1879, "Louisa is at the Bellevue writing her Art story in which some of my adventures will appear."[1] Portrayals of romantic painters and sculptors, particularly female artists, were common enough in Alcott's published works. But this particular story was never published even under a pseudonym: the untitled manuscript, written on blue letter paper, remained a part of the Alcott family papers in Houghton Library until almost one hundred years after Louisa first penned it at the Bellevue Hotel in Boston. The work was untitled but with the exception of our modern title of the tale, nothing has been added or omitted in this published edition. The mystery of its state as an unpublished and unnoticed manuscript both delights and puzzles Alcott's readers. To some extent this unpublished story is a reflection on the adulthood of May Alcott Neiriker. The example of her marriage and motherhood might have resolved for her sister the difficult choice between domestic life and career, but May's sudden death precluded such a resolution. Louisa never learned whether her sister could have overcome a central obstacle to the realization of women's human potential.

Alcott's audience appreciated the fact that her fiction was often based not only upon family folklore but, like all faithful social records, on the reality of culture and society as the writer experienced it. According to Sarah J. Hale, the editor of *Godey's Ladies Book*, "Miss Alcott has a faculty of entering into the lives and feelings of children that is conspicuously wanting in most writers who address them; and to this cause, to the consciousness among her readers that they are hearing about people like themselves, instead of abstract qualities with names, the popularity of her books is due."[2] This is true in the case of Alcott's adult fiction as well.

Diana and Persis Revealed

Once her writing had relieved the family of its earlier financial crises, Louisa Alcott often took a room in Boston or traveled farther to find a "room of her own" to write her fiction. When Alcott was beginning this art novel in 1879, she was also reading Mary Wollstonecraft, an eighteenth century women's rights theorist of radical reputation. The fact that Alcott considered her literary efforts almost entirely a labor of love for the support of her family and that she denied the need for self-actualization in the modern sense did not blind her to the fact that, in the mid-nineteenth century, the causes of domestic reform and women's rights had been united in what some historians have begun to call domestic feminism.

Aileen Kraditor has said, "What the feminists wanted has added up to something more fundamental than any specific set of rights of the sum total of all the rights that men have had; this fundamental something can perhaps be designated by the term autonomy."[3] She suggests that men have historically acted and been viewed as human beings who happen to be male and that women have been viewed historically as females who happen to be human. *Diana and Persis* explores the possibilities presented in the late nineteenth century for a new definition of woman's status and role. For Alcott and the leading characters of the novella, the search for this definition provoked a serious struggle between the domestic ideal of self-sacrifice and the conscious selfhood necessary to achieve the emancipation of women as human beings who happen to be female.

Persis, the young woman painter, is modeled closely upon Louisa's idealization of her sister May. Like May, Persis is funded by her family to study abroad and wins minor recognition in the Parisian art world. Devotion to art and devotion to home and family are both consuming vocations. Persis at first chooses art to the necessary exclusion of domestic life but, like Cecil in Alcott's earlier story, "The Marble Woman,"[4] Persis is a True Woman and cannot deny her heart's need. Cecil claimed, "Everything is possible to a woman when she loves," and May and her fictional counterpart Percy demand the right to both marital happiness and artistic success. It is significant that Alcott's female artists often denied the possibility of combining marriage and career and dedicated themselves to art only to reveal their "essential" nature in yielding to love. The process touches audiences because it is the assertion of a right to mature love once the discipline of formal training and the stresses of worldly competition have been worked through. In her earlier novels Alcott asserted repeatedly the necessity of adolescent experiences in self-reliance for young women. Only these experiences could prepare women to make the most serious choice the nineteenth century dictated to women: the choice of a husband. Countless fictional marriages faltered upon the childish irresponsibility of young brides who lacked both domestic and worldly experience. In *Diana and Persis*, Persis enjoys the separation from family and friend in a foreign land, struggling together with her artist-roommates to achieve individual distinction.

Her spirited defense of abolitionism reflects not only the entire Alcott family's dedication to antislavery but May's own painting of a black man for the Paris Salon. As a young, single woman she gallantly recalls the efforts of an earlier generation of antislavery women who had not been afraid to speak when public roles for women were forbidden. Persis/ May, breaking through the barriers against female artists, feels united with earlier, heroic groups of women abolitionists and artists.

Her friend Diana is aptly named for the goddess whose purity and devotion to virginal grace was actually discussed and debated by a circle of Transcendentalist luminaries, including Margaret Fuller and Ralph Waldo Emerson as well as Bronson Alcott and William Wetmore Story. They met in 1841, when Louisa was a young girl, to discuss the mythology of the Greeks and its expression in art, at the home of the Reverend George Ripley at Bedford Place in Boston. Emerson said that "the woodlands could tell us most about Diana," and the group remarked on the existence of two Dianas, the one pure and sacred to Athenians and the other, Diana of Ephesus, "whose orgies were not unusual, and who was considered as a bountiful mother rather than as a virgin huntress." The Transcendentalists, led by Margaret Fuller, laughed at the idea of a Diana said to be the mother of fifty sons and daughters and chose to discuss, of course, the Athenian Diana.[5] Louisa's Diana is the transcendental model. Though she toys briefly with the joys of foster motherhood, she seems to hold herself aloof, dedicated to a model of self-sacrifice to her art. As an artist she is undoubtedly modeled upon

Louisa May Alcott

Orchard House, the Alcott's home in Concord, Massachusetts

Puck, by Harriet Hosmer

Harriet Hosmer, a well known woman sculptor; as a woman she bears no small resemblance to Louisa Alcott herself.

Just as Diana is based on Hosmer, so the character of Stafford is clearly a fictionalized version of Hosmer's close friend, William Wetmore Story. The most renowned of the expatriate neo-classical sculptors, Story was the sometime friend of that colony of American women artists who settled on the seven hills of Rome in Louisa's girlhood like "a white marmorean flock,"[6] in the words of Henry James. They have been depicted most notably in Nathaniel Hawthorne's story, "The Marble Faun." Story and Hosmer are treated quite differently in the works of Hawthorne and Alcott. Unlike "The Marble Faun," written in 1859 which openly acknowledged both Hosmer's and Story's statues as models for those in the romance, Alcott's later tale does not mention the artists by name but does describe Hosmer's famous "Puck" and "Saul."

Story's relationship to Hosmer and to the other women in her circle, Emma Stebbins, Edmonia Lewis and the great actress Charlotte Cushman may give us a clue to why Alcott made Stafford/Story a widower and a man who had lost his "power" in her story. Charlotte Cushman, a mature, forceful woman, brought Hosmer to Rome and centered the "white marmorean flock" as a feminist group of artists. Story was enchanted with Harriet Hosmer as a talented child who needed the protection and encouragement of famous male artists and writers. Hosmer used her child-like persona to avoid any taint of fallen womanhood while pursuing a bohemian, artistic life. The defensive posture which reassured and attracted the male artists eventually repelled Cushman and her more assertive, forthright group. Story, while surely Hosmer's patron and master in her earlier career stage, had mixed feelings about the women artists as competitors, much as Hawthorne had his difficulties with the "damned mob of scribbling women," some of whom were actually members of his close circle.

Alcott's circle included the major figures in the artistic affairs of nineteenth century New Englanders who worked and studied abroad in London, Rome and Paris. Letters and visits flowed between all of them. For example, Cushman visited the Alcott home while Story participated in the famous classical conversations with Fuller, Bronson Alcott and Emerson.[7] Stafford and Diana are not only idealized portrayals of the two real artists — in addition, their fictional characters tell us much about the ambivalence Alcott continued to feel about women's lives and feelings. As a faithful social secretary she never resolved contradictions in fiction that she saw and experienced as unresolved in life. Nineteenth century men often felt most comfortable with unmarried women when they could treat them as children. An adult woman was supposed to be married and the mother of children. Those who chose spinsterhood and professions found frequently that they had to play at being children or else suffer the stigma assigned to partners in a "Boston marriage." Diana is chaste, and properly skeptical of close emotional attachments. Motherhood does tempt her, as we have seen, but any marriage would presumably resemble the celibate state depicted in "The Marble Woman," for while Stafford had lost his "power," his spiritual restoration was depicted only in terms of helping Diana to fame and his son to the possibility of a foster mother.

Diana and Persis' relationship avoids societal disapproval and brilliantly portrays a profound female friendship which in fiction and in nineteenth century

14

life provided affection, support and security to women in a society where the family was virtually the only source of such realizations. This friendship survives the strain of long separation and differing views about reconciling domesticity and artistic achievement. Diana, while fearful of her friend's marriage and its effects upon her career, wishes the best for Persis and does not shrink from enlarging her circle of affection to include her god-child and Persis' husband, August. If the character is generous and optimistic at the end of the novel, we must admit that the novelist was still skeptical. Persis, like May, insisted that her husband was more progressive than American men, and that her marriage must, perforce, be the model of a new sort of relationship. Alcott was quite clear, in all her works, that marriage and motherhood were synonymous, as indeed they certainly were well into the nineteenth century. It was motherhood that brooked no competitor in woman's heart and conscience. The dusty palette and Persis' reflection upon the next day's meal, while Diana and August discuss art, betray the narrative voice of Louisa May Alcott standing apart from her characters at the end.

If the family was the cornerstone of the Republic and motherhood the central obligation of women, then we can understand the difference between the lighthearted housekeeping of the female artist friends in their Paris apartment and the serious menu planning and family rituals of Persis and August in the novella. The artists, as single women, combine their domestic skills to make light of them, sharing tasks in order to get on with their careers. But the family requires an elaboration of domestic ritual to sustain its function in society. The family members do not define their relationship in terms of work external to the household, yet the household is no longer the workplace in the nineteenth century mode of production. Instead the family reproduces the citizenry both culturally and biologically, and it is women who play a central role in the family. Persis moves from the production of paintings outside of her Paris apartment to reproduction, biologically and culturally, within the conjugal apartment during the course of the story.

Diana has not been the creation of a male artist and owns her own heart as well as her own talent. She never for a moment denies the centrality of woman's domestic function in the maintenance of society, yet feels that she must deny that role personally lest she do it an injustice as a woman torn between work and domestic life. Like Cecil in "The Marble Woman," she does not deny the longings of the heart, but Diana is more self-reliant—able to cope with the realities of the larger world. Cecil is almost destroyed by an addiction to the opium, given by her male protector to still her womanly desire for warmth and affection. Diana needs no opiates and can sublimate her heart's needs to the demands of artistic work. Alcott's ability to deal with the world of woman's work is extraordinary because she understands the distinction between job and work in women's lives. It is work, the meaning of unalienated, disciplined activity that enables both Diana and Persis to find sisterhood and meaning in life.

While Persis is supported by her grandmother, Diana must struggle to support herself and to earn enough to fulfill her talent. The expenses of professional artists, while lower in Europe than America, were of enough concern even to May Alcott (largely supported by Louisa), to write a guide to aspiring young women on financial arrangements abroad.[8] In part, we are given to understand that Diana's struggles, like Louisa's, fitted her to sustain celibacy and self-worth. Percy's sense of her own capabilities and her drive to fulfill her talents are less sure, in part the result of what Alcott calls inherent nature and in part the result of life circumstances. Most nineteenth century people certainly believed in inherited temperament and Alcott's journals and novels attest to her own beliefs in that theory. But she was not ignorant of the differences produced by material circumstances of life as *Diana and Persis* demonstrates. May had been "fortune's favored child," while Louisa in her family's parlance was "duty's child."

> "What adversity had done for Diana, prosperity had done for Percy, and each drew from the soil of life the nourishment she needed, growing toward the sun of their desire slowly and steadily as green things struggle up in spring. The same aim was theirs, success and happiness; but with Diana success came first, with Percy happiness; both being conscious at times of that secret warfare of thwarted instincts and imperious ambitions, the demands of temperament as well as of talent, the lessons Nature teaches all of us in ways more mysterious and masterful than any one can give."

Perhaps one real fear intruded from Louisa May Alcott's life into the story—the fear of "the master passion which dissolves all lesser ties." The love of a man and woman by natural right, in Alcott's eyes, as in the eyes of the dominant society, transcended female friendship. Unless guarded against, this love could transcend woman's devotion to work. Men, it seemed, could work on despite full participation in the outside world; not only were they reinforced in their external role by their wives, but also they were able to cultivate emotional nondependence and impersonality. Women's reproductive roles were socially structured toward emotional dependency and an inability to sublimate personal concerns in work.

17

Yet Louisa Alcott did deal openly with her fears and in so doing did much to change the stereotype of emotional womanhood and rational manhood. Diana and Persis, while differing about the relationship between their artistic goals and emotional needs, both work to attain a professional fulfillment. In *Diana and Persis* Stafford is almost destroyed by his wife's death and is quite unable to work as a result. He cares for his young son and sets out to help Diana almost as a woman might help an aspiring young man to achieve his professional goals. August is frightened by Diana's effect upon his apparently domesticated wife, but he struggles with his feelings and Alcott openly portrays August and Diana as friendly rivals for Persis' commitment and energies. As a husband, August declared progressively that a new kind of marriage is possible, one which can enable a woman to have both domesticity and the fulfillment of work. He may be wrong, and the author is skeptical, but she presents the possibility and never denies the sincerity of the experiment.

Abba, Louisa and May

It is only in the examination of the Alcott family cycle that Louisa's sources for both optimism and skepticism become clear. In her mother's lifetime and in the years of her own youth, the model of self-sacrifice was a powerful one. In the late nineteenth century, spinsterhood became an increasingly honorable voluntary state justified by service to art, humanity or family. But subtle changes in the life cycle enabled a few daring women to demand both marriage and career and daring much, they risked estrangement from sisters and mothers who had sacrificed selves for the emancipation of future generations of women. Diana, the older friend, herein

represents Louisa's generation, "all the sad sisterhood," and Persis, the bright promise of May's
vanguard.

The antebellum generation of American feminists
included Abba May Alcott, and Louisa herself to some
extent. They were caught between the imperative to
promote the same sort of dependency and emotional
involvement in domestic roles with which they
themselves had been saddled and their desire to
prepare their daughters and sisters for emancipation.
In Louisa's fictional families and in her own life, we
find that families were set up to promote close
personal ties and emotional interdependence for
young women. Women who valued both family and
feminism had to develop a concept of individualism
and mutuality substantially different from the dominant ideal. Not only did the dominant ideology of
womanhood and the family demand the maintenance
of the home as refuge presided over by domestic,
dependent womanhood, but one of the unmistakable
signs of the achievement of social mobility for a family
was the presence of the wife and mother in her proper
place, the home. Women of the lower classes might
have to work but their labor was increasingly regarded
as transitory. Their elevation to the genteel status of
lady awaited only the conversion of individual members of the laboring poor to Christianity, which would
render them pious, thrifty, hard-working and ul-
timately deserving of social mobility. Evangelicals and
Liberals might argue over the means to redemption;
all were agreed that individual salvation was the key to
solving problems of poverty.

At the same time housework was real work and the
growth of factories and mills and railroads jeopardized
the fulfillment of middle class households' demands
for domestic servants. For a brief time Abba Alcott

ran an employment service and Louisa actually went "out into service" and eventually told a bitter tale of her exploitation in a short story.[9] At the other end of the spectrum, her own experience did not make Louisa any more sympathetic to Irish servant girls whom she regarded as a dull and hopeless lot. Women of the middle classes found themselves doing more and more housework as household technology remained primitive in a period when industrialization linked progress to new aspirations for individual mobility in the dominant society.

Bronson Alcott played a somewhat ambivalent role in the debates between liberal theologians' support of principles including women's suffrage and a more public role for women and conservative exponents of the family's crucial role in societal stability. As a leading exponent of the importance of moral education, Bronson carefully recorded the birth of each daughter in his journal. On July 26, 1840 when May was born, he declared that a fourth female child obviously manifested God's will that the Alcotts be content to "rear women for the future world." Abba May Alcott was received by the family as "a proud little Queen," the last baby of the family. Like her mother, she was to be the youngest daughter of her family. The Alcotts acknowledged an end to their mother's childbearing role with May's birth. Whether this was a voluntary decision or a recognition of Mrs. Alcott's age (she was 40 years old) and consequent infertility we do not know. Bronson had publicly urged that husbands restrain their sexual impulses in favor of their wives' health and well-being. Such declarations implied a growing autonomy and power for women in the family indicating the tremendous influence and even control through moral persuasion exercised by Abba Alcott over her daughters and, to a certain extent, her husband. Whether voluntary or not, the effect of this end to childbearing was that May became the beloved and admittedly spoiled pet of the family, much like Persis who is doted upon by a loving grandmother.

The eight year difference between Louisa and May sufficed to soften May's experience of a disastrous communal experiment, "Fruitlands," recalled by Louisa in a bitterly satirical essay, "Transcendental Wild Oats."[10] Bronson Alcott and an English, Owenite-Socialist, Charles Lane, attempted an extended family community on a wildly improbable economic base of non-exploitative agriculture. In their concern for the exclusion of black slave labor products, animal beasts of burden, and even land exploitation, they thoughtlessly exploited Abba Alcott and Louisa as domestic servants. The women worked unceasingly, sewing by the light of the hearthfire because whale oil, and even candles made of tallow were forbidden. The entire family was close to starvation and freezing before the experiment ended. But by the time May was old enough to demand art lessons and to long for pretty clothes, both Louisa and Anna were out working to support themselves and both sent money home. Anna especially doted on May, but after the elder sister's marriage to John Pratt, Louisa took up the sometimes difficult role of May's protector and benefactor.

Louisa's self-conscious attitude toward May was partly sisterly and partly maternal. She seemed to rejoice in fitting the younger girl up as a queen and in accentuating the differences between her own life and May's. The age difference between May and Louisa is just enough, when taken with the fact of May's position as the favorite and "baby," to suggest some differences in the life expectations of young women before and after the Civil War. In May's adolescence, education and professional training for women together with the curiously contradictory effects of domestic feminism combined to make young womanhood a more serious stage. Louisa had argued for its importance in her novels but her sister was the recipient of its blessings.

Adolescence was no longer just a period of potential seduction and disgrace to foolish females; it was becoming a time of serious preparation for wifehood and motherhood. Since women's burdens were prestigiously increased as men left much of child-rearing and moral standard bearing to them, women demanded better education in ways hitherto reserved to men. Moreover within the Alcotts' own walls, Abba's journals and letters record the women's determined effort toward stability and economic security. In part, as noted, Louisa's and Anna's incomes enabled Abba to bring May up in a more comfortable manner. But also, cultural validation of decision-making as necessary to the role of wife and mother strengthened Abba's hand at home. (Bronson's tendency to put his principles before material well-being had been accepted, with plenty of tears and protests, during the first years of their marriage.) It may well have been the Alcott family's espousal of domestic reform that enabled Abba and the girls to exercise more decision-making power within the home. The second half of *Little Women* had openly remarked on the feminine domination of the "March family." The second half of the Alcott family history echoed the author's insight.

Since girls and young women were becoming more important within the family structure, their talents and dreams could be taken more seriously. It was not the women's movement alone, in the sense of political struggles, that aided May's ambitions so much as the hidden feminist implications of women's increasing importance in the family. Her artistic abilities were given every opportunity to develop, sometimes through the aegis of family friends and increasingly through Louisa's earned income.

For example, Daniel Smith French, who received his first lump of clay and tools from May, recalled her attendance at two Boston art studios, one taught by William Hunt, in drawing and painting and "conducted much like the Beaux Arts in Paris. A studio was provided where the students worked from casts or still life or living models. . . . These classes were exclusively for women."[11] At the same time May studied with Dr. Rimmer, described by Van Wyck Brooks as a fascinating and gifted sculptor and draftsman.[12] Louisa recalled his physical presence, complete with German accent, in the character of Dr. Frederick Bhaer, husband of "Jo March." Both teachers were professional artists of some reputation and the training received in their studios was serious. Although women had been free to write fiction for some time, there was, as numerous critics have noted, no professional training required for such work. It was something a gifted woman could do as a pastime or to earn a living, but society need not lower many barriers to accommodate the "scribbling women." Women found increasing acceptance in the art world, first in Europe and later in America; Hunt's female classes were the only life drawing classes available in the Boston area for a few years. Rimmer's classes were still more innovative because they were open to men and women together and attempted to convey some serious knowledge of anatomy. How serious the acceptance of women as career artists was has not yet been examined.

By 1868, May was able to give drawing lessons herself and Louisa shared her room at No. 6 Hayward Place with her sister. The "light housekeeping" arrangement pleased the usually solitary, writing sister very much. She found herself on the fringe of a sociable group of May's friends and behaved very much like the wise old spinsters in her novels, dispensing advice and comfort to May's little circle. For two years, Louisa was able to refer to herself and May as "the workers," though May insisted on enjoying herself in the process. The young artist did the illustrations for the first edition of *Little Women* and was the model not only for "Amy" in what became the *Little Women* trilogy *(Little Women, Little Men* and *Jo's Boys)* but also "Polly" in *An Old Fashioned Girl.* The two sisters moved three times between 1868 and 1870, with May preferring the fashionable Hotel Bellevue and Louisa choosing quieter furnished rooms in which to scribble. Their shared experience was a productive one for Louisa; she finished *An Old Fashioned Girl* in her usual haste, but without the exhaustion and illness that often accompanied her writing.

It is important to remark here that marriage and motherhood are inescapably linked in all of Alcott's work. Once a woman accepts the love of a man she will owe her first allegiance to childbearing and it is this fact which makes spinsterhood the preferred status for the first generation of emancipated women. That such a choice will not make the spinsters "unwomanly" is important, too. Louisa is simply unsure of the frontiers of marital relationships at this point. Her own father had been outspoken about family limitations, and although he was frequently oblivious of his family's material needs he was not necessarily bound by his masculinity to disdain housewifely functions. Bronson did cook, at least when the children were small, and he did mind the Alcott girls when they were very young. But certainly Abba had the primary care of household and children, and at least while Anna and Louisa were small she was exhausted and terribly anxious about finances and about Bronson's eccentric experiments in education and living arrangements. It took Bronson's withdrawal and collapse after "Fruitlands" failed to force Abba into a dominant managerial role.

The combination of Bronson's avowed respect for domestic skills and his outspoken support of women's rights might have been enough to make Louisa comfortable with the ideal of a new kind of marriage as well as a new kind of woman but for one significant fact: Abba Alcott's example of long suffering and not so silent motherhood. Marriage and motherhood had obviously given Louisa's mother both great satisfaction and great frustration. Her letters and journals attest to a mind at least as capable of intellectual insight as Bronson's but with little opportunity to develop in a disciplined fashion. She seems to have been a very talented woman — her writing is often livelier, more pungent and evocative then either Bronson's or Louisa's. But despite Bronson's domestic and feminist principles, the women closest to him, his wife and daughters, were constrained by their feminine domestic roles. May, the youngest, suffered the least from the constraint and was indeed a "lucky child" as her sister called her. She was a young woman in a period of expanding possibilities; the domestic virtues of her mother and sisters, including that of self-sacrifice, served her advancement well.

Louisa's success enabled her to go to Europe with May and their friend Alice Bartlett just after the publication of *An Old Fashioned Girl*. The trip was a great success, as Louisa's letters and May's sketches sent home attest. Louisa celebrated the entire trip in her *Shawl Straps* and *Aunt Jo's Scrap Bag.*[13] Much of the comedy in these tales concerns the juxtaposition of independent American spinsters with imprisoned European girls. The latter are forever planning trousseaus or venturing out to shop with watchful mammas, prompting Louisa to sign letters, "Spinsterhood Forever."

Probably no other time was as happy for Louisa Alcott, and from Dinan, in France, she wrote home, "May is well and jolly and very good to her crooky old sister."[14] They wandered and explored and worried a bit about the outbreak of the Franco-Prussian War. Finally Louisa worked on *Little Men* early in 1871 while still abroad. The sisters had received the news of John Pratt's death, and Louisa wrote with the explicit motive of earning money for Anna's now fatherless sons. May remained in London to complete her art training for at least a year, while Louisa returned home to deal with the latest family crisis.

By fall she was exhausted from coping with her mother's poor health and Anna's bereavement. May came home and the entire family celebrated Louisa's and her father's joint birthday together for two more years. During this period, May took Louisa's place, nursing first her mother and then Anna, and it looked as though there might indeed be the "sisterhood" as imagined in *An Old Fashioned Girl.* But in the spring of 1873, after finishing *Work*, Louisa typically gave up the "writing room" of her own in Boston returning to Concord to take up the domestic task alone. She sent May back to Europe with one thousand dollars to continue her art training, though surely she undoubtedly expected her sister to return.

The letters from Europe were once again enthusiastic. Though May was 33, she sounded like a young girl; her housekeeping arrangements were described as more like playing house than any serious responsibility. She was a student, and not at all concerned about fashion, European galleries, and good food. Among other things, May wrote about

> "another advantage which my artistic sister will appreciate as I do. Shops abound with cheap clothing of all sorts, ready made. Work's also so cheap that a young woman of moderate means can get up a neat and handsome wardrobe for half the sum it costs at home."[15]

May continued to detail her pleasures in a delightful way but still like her sister Louisa, she took care to hedge each self-indulgence with a list of work accomplished.

May had a strong appreciation for European culture and wished that America would have good collections of pictures, free to all "where any beggar may solace himself with beauty if so inclined."[16] Her copies of Turner won John Ruskin's praise and she was learning to turn out "pot boilers" as her sister empathetically termed them, to pay her own way. Louisa noted, somewhat enviously, that the 33 year old "thrifty child" was "very happy in her success." For May, success meant self-fulfillment and independence which involved far less self-sacrifice than Louisa demanded of herself.

Like an indulgent but self-pitying mother, Louisa wanted proof that May saw her duty, even when abroad working as an artist. She demanded May's recognition of the bittersweet female sacrifice of her benefactor, and then she let the younger girl go out to play. May returned in 1874 to find Louisa's health seriously deteriorating. She suffered increasingly severe rheumatism and blinding headaches, but kept writing stories for children, as well as advice columns

in the *New York Ledger.* At this point, Louisa referred
to herself as "the golden goose who can sell her eggs
for a good price if she isn't killed by too much
driving."[17] In the spring of 1876 the family agreed to
send May back to Europe. Louisa wrote of this
decision, "She cannot find the help she needs here and
is happy and busy in her own world over there. God
be with her, she has done her distasteful duty
faithfully and deserves a reward."[18]

The Alcotts' contemporaries and their biographers
have noted, that, when May did her duty she was
rewarded with her freedom but Louisa's reward

> "after all, was that which came from the delight of
> giving. For her, the line of duty was the only line
> she visualized, and she followed it ungrudgingly.
> For May, the line of beauty ever beckoned, and she
> must tread its graceful curves; so they all felt, so
> May believed."[19]

This time May went back to Europe and never
returned to Concord. She established herself for a
while in Paris. There, living close to several other
American women artists, she worked under Monsieur
Krug on the Boulevard Clichy. It was a women's
studio that allowed nude models and encouraged
criticism of the students' work by leading painters.
May carefully listed which male artists would receive
ladies and which would not. Interestingly she paid
homage to "a band of American ladies some years ago,
who supported one another with such dignity and
modesty, in a steadfast purpose,"[20] the purpose being
the acquisition of life drawing skills in a mixed class of
art students. She was quite sure that it was the
American females' unique attributes of courage and
"simple earnestness and purity" which had won a
right, regrettably withdrawn by the time May was
studying in Paris. The female artists, she said,

contrasted favorably with the conventional image of husband-hunting American girls abroad.

May's letters describe the comfortable and supportive group of young female artists, sharing breakfasts, Thanksgiving dinners far from home, and not least of all sharing ambition. "Kate," "Rose" and "May" were referred to as "three jolly spinsters" and their simplified housekeeping arrangements and easygoing hours were experienced by Louisa only in her imaginative re-creation of her sister's life. Conscious of her mother's and sister's intense interest in the minute details of a female artist abroad, May obliged them with sketches and descriptions, including a verbal portrait of the successful Mary Cassatt whose teas were a mecca for young American artists in Paris. The Parisian experiences were clearly bases for Persis' fictional adventures in Alcott's "Art story."

By 1876, Abba Alcott's health was failing, but she faithfully copied bits of May's letters into her Journal. She took pride in her daughter's accomplishments, but still referred to her as "a good child." Meanwhile, the child was "making plans to stay in Europe having proved to my satisfaction that there is enough talent to pay for educating it and giving my life to it." At the same time, May reassured the family that she could make an occasional summer visit home, "if you want me very much;" or better yet, "why not shut up Apple Slump for a year and let Nan have all the pretty things and a general pick and let Lu come for a year's vacation, if Mother continues well and can spare her."[21]

The tug of war continued with a silken cord between Concord and Paris for a year. When May gently hinted at permanent expatriation during her "Paris excursion," Abba said, "I think she has realized what a sacrifice to me it has been to have her gone so far, and has conscientiously tried to gratify me and her sisters by these frequent and interesting accounts of her progress in art."[22.]

May had a still life praised by Monsieur Muller who urged her to send it to the Salon. The date of the exhibition was duly noted along with a marvelous tale of the young women rushing to finish their work, sharing a "jolly breakfast" while "such a merry artistic set was never seen before."[23] May's painting was accepted and her mother recorded her success. Moreover, Bronson sent May a note of congratulations in red ink, "the color that best represents your success."

On her 77th birthday, Abba Alcott penned her last words, a notation of "the coming of May's letter full of pleasant news."[24] She died a few days later and her daughters' loss, particularly Louisa's, was more intense than the natural loss suffered by adult children at a parent's death. Abba Alcott represented a wholly sympathetic support for independence while still binding her daughters to their parental family, a classic example of the "modified extended family" which may well have vanished in the last decade of the nineteenth century. As Abba's health was clearly failing, Louisa had sorrowfully observed that "Marmee came back to herself, but sadly feeble — never to be our brave, energetic leader any more."[25]

So May went on with her work and at one point suggested that the spinster devotion to art would justify her independence by evoking images of self-sacrifice to justify her artistic dreams: "If mine can't be a happy domestic life such as I have longed and prayed for, perhaps the good God meant me for great things in other ways."[26] Then, "Perhaps this sacrifice I have freely chosen to make in losing one year of Marmee's life may make me work better."[27] It was a strange way of comparing Louisa's years of setting aside both serious work and pleasure to minister to her family to May's insistence on her own work and independence before filial devotion. May turned self-sacrifice on its head and insisted that she had sacrificed going home for the work which was in itself a great sacrifice—for art.

Yet one month later May was happily at work, in new quarters and with a new male admirer. This "nice Swiss" was Ernest Neiriker, a handsome young businessman, 14 years younger than May. She married him four months after her mother's death. There are several obvious reasons why she married just when she did and why she married Ernest Neiriker. First, her letter announcing her engagement (March 11, 1878) was immediately followed by another letter (March 24, 1878) announcing their marriage.[26] Ostensibly her fiancé's business had called him to move from London to Paris. May's announcement of a *fait accompli* precluded any resistance to the marriage by the Alcotts.

Secondly, since May was by all accounts the most physically attractive sister, never lacking in suitors, why had she waited so long to marry if a "happy domestic life" was what she wanted? The answer may well be that she also wanted a career as an artist and that her mother's paradoxical position on women's domestic imperatives and women's rights, combined with sister Louisa's choice of spinsterhood, all proved too weighty a precedent. May went to Europe, thereby achieving some physical and psychic distance from family support and family hindrance to her life. She was finally free, with Abba's death, to claim the rights of a "new woman." Persis too, regrets her grandmother's death but must put a great distance between family and friend to achieve a new status.

May wanted Louisa to come to stay with them, but she firmly and bluntly indicated that although conscious of sisterly obligations and affections she would not be deterred from pursuing her chosen life. Not only was Louisa not to hinder May's plans, but the constraints of American society and its conventional expectations of women were to be rejected.

"Not a wish seems ungratified except that Louisa is not well enough to come and see and enjoy my good fortune with me ... She must not think my own happiness has made me unmindful of her, for it only draws us nearer. But I have laid out my future life and hope not to swerve from purpose. I do not mean to be hindered by envious people, or anything to divert me from accomplishing my dream ... For myself this simple artistic life is so charming, that America seems death to all aspiration or hope of work ... It is the perfection of living; the wife so free from household cares, so busy and so happy. I never mean to have a house or many belongings, but lead the delightfully free life I do now with no society to bother me, and nothing to prevent my carrying out my aims ..."[29]

Again, Louisa must have tried to evoke in May a recollection of circumstances in Concord by dwelling on Abba's death and her own bereavement.[30] Anna was busy with her sons and even Bronson had succeeded on his own. But May resisted any guilt over her own new life. Louisa did find some solace in the struggle for suffrage in Concord, but even this did not sustain her; she was ill and depressed and when she tried to respond to May's invitations, she had to write, "at the last moment gave it up, fearing to undo all the good this weary year of ease has done for me and be a burden on her." She had compared May's life to her own,

"How different our lives are just now—I so lonely, sad and sick; she so happy, well and blest. She

always had the cream of things and deserved it. My
time is yet to come . . . I dawdle about and wait to
see if I am to live or die. If I live it will be for some
new work . . . I wonder what?"[31]

But Louisa recovered and by some strange irony it
was May who died a few weeks after the birth of her
child, Louisa May Neiriker. While May was pregnant
and busily completing seven pictures for exhibition,
Louisa had begun "an art novel, with May's romance
as its theme."[32] That may well have been the untitled
manuscript of four chapters we shall call *Diana and
Persis.* May's death not only left her sister unable to
write of her for some time, it left her life's goal
unresolved in Louisa's eyes. May had demanded both
marriage and career; Louisa was prepared that
fortune's favorite child should be so blest but she had
also been curious as to just how May would manage
this feat.

May left her daughter to Louisa's care and in the fall
of 1880 Lulu arrived in America. Ednah Cheney tells
us that for Louisa, ". . . the principle interest of the
next few years was the care of this child. This new care
and joy helped to fill up the void in her life . . ."
Certainly baby Diana is to be the god-child of Persis'
dearest friend, as Louisa Neiriker was Louisa May
Alcott's ward.

Louisa's skepticism about marriage and a career
may certainly have been more than the idiosyncratic
result of her experience in the Alcott family. Between
1846 and 1880 a small but significant rise in the
percentage of unmarried American women occurred.
Although, some of these women simply did not
survive long enough to be married, Daniel Smith
observes that ". . . the numerically tiny minority who
remained single had far larger historical significance
than their numbers would suggest,"[33] and further that
"the rise in spinsterhood among those born in the last

four decades of the nineteenth century may not have been surprising . . . in the context of the tides of the woman's movement." There were new educational and vocational opportunities for women during and after the Civil War and, as Louisa Alcott repeatedly noted, these opportunities were best seized by spinsters.

The real problem, however, still lay in finding a way to combine marriage, motherhood, and expanded opportunities for women. May Alcott tried to solve the problem by marrying later than women usually did and to a liberated foreign gentleman of some ambition. She was outspoken in her analysis of her mother's problems as stemming from Bronson's anti-materialism or perhaps to his rather stubborn persistence. Certainly Louisa agreed with her sister that financial independence made life much easier and to that end Louisa devoted much of her adult life. But something about this kind of individual, pragmatic solution did not satisfy Louisa as easily as it did May. May chose expatriation and was not, so far as we know, particularly involved with the Women's Movement. But Louisa was deeply involved in it and she recognized that although women were a class, in one sense, they were also affected by the woman problem in varying ways according to their economic and social positions.

Abba Alcott had succeeded in convincing her daughters that domestic skills were necessary and worthy of some pride, but she never quite succeeded in convincing them or herself that these tasks were particularly pleasurable. All of them heartily detested the kitchen; Abba had said that if ever she lived alone (an impossible dream) she would subsist on apples and cereal rather than cook. Louisa was happiest with a competent housekeeper, while constantly complaining of the problems of finding and keeping one. She did housework herself in great bursts of self-sacrifice and then retreated to hotels and rooming houses to write. May's great joy in Paris was an apartment free of heavy carpets, stairs and elaborate furniture. She made a great point of mentioning the bare, polished, easily swept floors and convenient housekeeping setup she enjoyed in Europe. When marriage dictated a more elaborate lifestyle she shamelessly relied upon a French maid-of-all-work and painted away all day, going for moonlit strolls with Ernest in the evening, just as Persis and her August promenaded in Louisa's novella.

The virtue of orderly housekeeping is a thread through many of Alcott's books, but one must be careful here not to accuse Alcott of claiming that domesticity was "natural" to women. On the contrary, she suggests that woman can be born, like Diana, with "masculine" needs for recognition. But in several novels she also suggested that the best men, like Uncle Alex in *Rose in Bloom* and *Eight Cousins*, could sew on their own buttons, cook and tend to children and that it was these men who especially appreciated women. When the sculptor Stafford in *Diana and Persis* suggested that Diana's sculpture embodied the best in a "fine man and a fine woman working together," the most obvious message was that works of art, images of man's perfectibility, are works of genius when they combine the best of masculine and feminine virtues.

In short, Alcott generally suggested that life would do better to imitate art in resolving the woman question. One way of dealing with the problem of gender role definition was to suggest that women be given an opportunity to develop their masculine talents while retaining their traditional skills. These skills, acquired as they were through centuries of family example, inculcated values of devotion, service to others and attention to the humble details of sustenance, which did in fact mark women as a class.

The traits which marked woman as a class were both ennobling and imprisoning. Such characteristics could remain enriching while losing their negative constraints if men learned tenderness, domestic service and humility from women's example. But the contradiction between those traits needed to embody the womanly or domestic ideal and those needed for worldly achievement were never fully resolved by Alcott in her own life and were only speculatively resolved in her fiction. After May's death, Louisa took on the care of her daughter and for a time seemed to embody her own preconceived judgment that mothers were too preoccupied with maternal cares to create much else besides a future generation. Still, she did find governesses for Lulu and she did continue writing, though her production was certainly diminished.

Louisa was truly ambivalent about dependency and independence for women. She was fearful of the implications of May's struggle for the best of both worlds. Her hesitation in visiting her sister in France and the implication in May's letters that Louisa regarded her marriage as a violation of either the vestal virgin's oath to art or as a violation of the charge to care for the Alcotts must be taken quite seriously. Louisa rallied in mental and physical health every time she was called upon to resume work in the name of duty to others. Once she had provided for her family in every way, she faltered in strength and purpose. The circumstances of her death gave some indication that those virtues that sustained self-sacrifice and duty could be in contradiction to those attributes necessary for autonomy.

Diana and Persis, with its themes and variations still vital, comes to our attention almost one hundred years after it was written. The contradictions it depicts have not been resolved — they reach out to us, full of resonance in our own lives. Domesticity is still defined as "woman's work" and women still long for fulfillment as human beings.

FOOTNOTES

1. Madeleine B. Stern, *Louisa May Alcott*, New York, 1957, p. 275.
   I am grateful also to Professor Jeanne Stump, University of Kansas, for the direct reference in May Alcott's diary entry in January 28, 1879 and for her shared enthusiasm in the discovery of *Diana and Persis*.

2. Hale's comment was used as an advertisement by Roberts Brothers in the second edition frontispiece of Louisa May Alcott, *Work: A Story of Experience*.

3. Aileen Kraditor, *Up From the Pedestal: Selected Writings in American Feminism*, New York, 1968.

4. Madeleine B. Stern, ed., *Plots and Counterplots: More Unknown Thrillers of Louisa May Alcott*, pp. 131-238.

5. Caroline Healey Dall, *Margaret and Her Friends or Ten Conversations with Margaret Fuller Upon the Mythology of the Greeks and Its Expression in Art, Beginning March 1, 1841*, Boston, 1895, p. 119.

6. The story of the "White Marmorean Flock" remains to be analyzed in its entirety. Excellent sources on the individuals involved in the expatriate colony and examples of their work are:
   Joseph Leach, *Bright Particular Star, The Life and Times of Charlotte Cushman*, New Haven and London, 1970.
   Margaret Farrand Thorp, *The Literary Sculptors*, North Carolina, 1965.
   Henry James, *William Wetmore Story*, Volumes I and II,

Edinburgh and London, 1903.
Cornelia Curred, *Harriet Hosmer, Letters and Memories*, New York, 1912.
Eleanor Tufts, *Our Hidden Heritage; Five Centuries of Women Artists*, New York, 1974.

7. Ednah D. Cheney, ed., *Louisa May Alcott, Her Life, Letters, and Journals*, Boston, 1889.

8. May Alcott, *Studying Art Abroad.*

9. Louisa May Alcott, "How I Went Out Into Service; A Story," *The Independent*, XXVI, June 4, 1874. The incidents are further developed in Louisa May Alcott, *Work: A Story of Experience*, Boston, 1873.

10. Louisa May Alcott, "Transcendental Wild Oats," *The Independent*, Volume XXV, No. 1307 (December 18, 1873); reprinted in *The Woman's Journal*, Volume V, No. 8 (February 21, 1874).

11. Daniel Smith French, preface to Caroline Ticknor, *May Alcott, A Memoir*, Boston, 1927.

12. Van Wyck Brooks, *The Dream of Arcadia, American Writers and Artists in Italy*, 1760-1915.

13. Louisa May Alcott, "Shawl Straps," *The Christian Union*, Volume V, Nos. 12, 13, 14. Alcott, *Aunt Jo's Scrap Bag*, Volume I, Boston, Roberts Brothers, 1872.

14. Ticknor, *May Alcott: A Memoir.*

15. Ibid., p. 105.

16. Ibid.

17. Ibid., p. 120.

18. Ibid.

19. Ibid.

20. Ibid., p. 125.

21. Ibid., p. 126.

22. Ibid., p. 127.

23. Ibid., p. 128.

24. Ibid., p. 248.

25. Cheney, *Life, Letters and Journals*, p. 271.

26. Ibid.

27. Ibid.

28. Ticknor, *May Alcott: A Memoir*, pp. 258-261.

29. Ibid., p. 267.

30. Ibid.

31. Cheney, *Life, Letters and Journals*, p. 317.

32. Ibid.

33. Daniel Scott Smith, "Family Limitation, Sexual Control and Domestic Feminism in Victorian America," in Mary Hartman and Lois W. Banner, ed., *Clio's Consciousness Raised*, New York, 1975, pp. 119-136.

BIBLIOGRAPHY

Alcott, Amos Bronson. *Concord Days*. Boston: Roberts Brothers, 1888.

——. *Essays on Education*, ed. by Walter Hardins. Gainesville, Florida: Scholars' Facsimiles and Reprints, 1960.

——. *Sonnets and Canzonets*. Boston: Roberts Brothers, 1882.

——. *Table Talk*. Boston: Roberts Brothers, 1877.

——. *The Journals of Bronson Alcott*, selected and edited by Odell Shepard. Boston: Little, Brown & Co., 1938.

Alcott, Louisa May. [Primary sources used in this study are listed in chronological order by date of publication or by date of manuscript if unpublished. A more complete list of Louisa May Alcott's published works appears in Madeleine B. Stern's *Louisa May Alcott*.]

——. "The Rival Painters. A Face of Rome." *Olive Branch*, XVII (September, 1851).

——. "The Rival Prima Donnas" (by Florence Fairfield [pseudonym]). *Saturday Evening Gazette*, Series for 1854 (November 1, 1854).

——. *Flower Fables*. Boston: George W. Briggs, 1855.

——. "A New Years Blessing." *Saturday Evening Gazette*, Quarto Series, January 5, 1856.

——. "The Sisters' Trial." *Saturday Evening Gazette*, Quarto Series, January 26, 1856.

——. "Little Genevieve." *Saturday Evening Gazette*, Quarto Series, March 29, 1856.

43

——. "The Lady and the Woman." *Saturday Evening Gazette*, Quarto Series, October 4, 1856.

——. "With a Rose, That Bloomed on the Day of John Brown's Martyrdom" (poem). *The Liberator*, XXX, January 20, 1860.

——. "Love and Self Love." *The Atlantic Monthly*, V (March, 1860).

——. "A Modern Cinderella: or, The Little Old Shoe." *The Atlantic Monthly*, VI (October, 1860).

——. "M.L." *The Commonwealth*, I, January 24, 31 & February 7, 14, 22, 1863.

——. "Hospital Sketches." *The Commonwealth*, I, May 22, 29 & June 12, 26, 1863.

——. *Hospital Sketches*. Boston: James Redpath, 1863.

——. "Thoreau's Flute" (poem). *Atlantic Monthly*, XII (September, 1863).

——. "My Contraband; or, The Brothers." *The Atlantic Monthly*, XII (November, 1863). Reprinted in *Camp and Fireside Stories*.

——. "A Hospital Christmas." *The Commonwealth*, II, January 8 & 15, 1864.

——. "A Golden Wedding: and What Came of It." *The Commonwealth*, II, April 29 & May 6, 1864.

——. "Colored Soldiers' Letters." *The Commonwealth*, II, July 1, 1864.

——. "Nelly's Hospital." *Our Young Folks*, I (April, 1865).

——. *Moods*. Boston: Loring, 1865.

——. "Behind a Mask: or, A Woman's Power." *The Flag of Our Union*, XXI, October 13, 20, 27 & November 3, 1866.

——. "Merry's Monthly Chat with His Friends." *Merry's Museum*, I and II, January, 1868-December, 1869.

——. "Happy Women." *The New York Ledger*, XXIV, April 11, 1868.

——. "Mr. Emerson's Third Lecture." *National Anti-Slavery Standard*, XXIX, October 31, 1868.

——. "Report on the Radical Club." *National Anti-Slavery Standard*, XXIX, October 31, 1868.

——. *Little Women or, Meg, Jo, Beth and Amy.* Boston: Roberts, 1868.

——. *Little Women or Meg, Jo, Beth and Amy.* Part Second. Boston: Roberts, 1869.

——. *Hospital Sketches and Camp and Fireside Stories.* Boston: Roberts, 1869.

——. *An Old Fashioned Girl.* Boston: Roberts Bros., 1870.

——. *Little Men: Life at Plumfield with Jo's Boys.* London, Sampson Low, 1871.

——. *My Boys. Aunt Jo's Scrap Bag.* Boston: Roberts Bros., 1872.

——. *Shawl Straps. Aunt Jo's Scrap Bag, II.* Roberts Bros., 1872.

——. "Letter to John Hart." Cornell University Regional History Archives, 1872.

——. "Work; or Christie's Experiment." *Christian Union*, VI & VII, 1873.

——. *Work: A Story of Experience.* Boston: Roberts Bros., 1873.

——. "How I Went Out Into Service. A Story." *The Independent*, XXVI, June 4, 1874.

——. "Letter of Miss Louisa Alcott." *The Woman's Journal*, V, Nov. 14, 1874.

——. "Woman's Part in the Concord Celebration." *The Woman's Journal*, VI, May 1, 1875.

——. *Eight Cousins; or The Aunt-Hill.* Boston: Roberts Bros., 1875.

——. "A Visit to the Tombs." *The Youth's Companion*, XLIX, May 25, 1876.

——. "Letter from Louisa M. Alcott." *The Woman's Journal,* VII, July 15, 1876.

——. *Rose in Bloom. A Sequel to "Eight Cousins."* Boston: Roberts Bros., 1876.

——. *A Modern Mephistopheles.* Boston: Roberts Bros., 1877. (No Name Series)

——. *Under the Lilacs.* Boston: Roberts Bros., 1878.

——. "Letter from Louisa M. Alcott." *The Woman's Journal,* XI, April 3, 1880.

——. "Letter from Louisa M. Alcott." *The Woman's Journal,* XIII, Feb. 11, 1882.

——. "W.C.T.U. of Concord." *Concord Freeman,* X, June 30, 1882.

——. "R. W. Emerson." *Demorest's Monthly Magazine,* XVIII, (July, 1882).

——. *Moods. A Novel* (Revised edition). Boston: Roberts Bros., 1882.

——. Preface to *Prayers by Theodore Parker.* Boston: Roberts Bros., 1882.

——. "Letter from Miss Alcott." *The Woman's Journal,* XIV, March 10, 1883.

——. "In Memoriam Sophia Foord." *The Woman's Journal,* XVI, April 11, 1885.

——. "Miss Alcott on Mind Cure." *The Woman's Journal,* XVI, April 18, 1885.

——. "Kind Words from Miss Alcott." *The Woman's Journal,* XVI, May 16, 1885.

——. "When Shall Our Young Women Marry?" *The Brooklyn Magazine,* IV, April, 1886.

——. "The Lay of a Golden Goose" (poem). *The Woman's Journal,* XVII, May 8, 1886.

——. *Jo's Boys and How They Turned Out. A Sequel to "Little Men."* Boston: Roberts Bros., 1886.

——. "A Flower Fable." *The Woman's Journal,* XVIII, Feb. 26, 1887.

——. "Early Marriages." *The Ladies Home Journal*, IV, Sept. 1887.

——. *A Modern Mephistopheles and a Whisper in the Dark*. Boston: Roberts Bros., 1889.

——. *Recollections of My Childhood's Days*. London: Sampson Low, 1890.

——. *Louisa May Alcott, Life, Letters and Journals*, ed. by Ednah D. Cheney. Boston: Roberts Bros., 1892.

Alcott, John S. P. *Little Women Letters from the House of Alcott*, selected by Jessie Bonstelle, Marian DeForest. Boston: Little, Brown & Co., 1914.

Alcott, Louisa May. "Diana & Persis." Four chapter, untitled fragmentary manuscript, Houghton Library, Cambridge, Mass.

Alcott Papers, Houghton Library, Cambridge, Mass., marked 59 M-309, 59 M-310, 59 M-312, and 59 M-313.

Alcott, William A. *The Young Housekeeper*. Boston: Geo. W. Light, 1839.

——. *The Young Mother*. Boston: Light & Stearns, 1836.

——. *The Young Wife*. Boston: George W. Light, 1837.

Anthony, Katharine. *Louisa May Alcott*. New York: Alfred A. Knopf, 1938.

Anthony, Susan B., Matilda Joslyn Sage and Elizabeth Cady Stanton. *History of Woman Suffrage*. III, 1876-1885. Rochester, N.Y.: Charles Mann, 1887.

Baylor, Ruth M. *Elizabeth Palmer Peabody, Kindergarten Pioneer*. Phila.: Univ. of Penn. Press, 1965.

Banner, Lois W. "On Writing Women's History." *The Journal of Interdisciplinary History*, II, Autumn, 1971.

Benston, Margaret. "The Political Economy of Women's Liberation." *Monthly Review*, September, 1969.

Bloomberg, Susan E., Mary Frank Fox, Robert M. Warner, Sam Bass Warner, Jr. "A Census Probe into Nineteenth Century Family History: Southern Michigan, 1850-1880." *Journal of Social History*, V, Fall, 1971.

47

Boas, Ralph. "The Romantic Lady." *Romanticism in America*, ed. by George Boas. Baltimore: 1940.

Bode, Carl. *The Anatomy of American Popular Culture, 1840-1861*. Berkeley: Univ. of Calif. Press, 1960.

Bridges, William E. "Family Patterns and Social Values in America, 1825-1875." *American Quarterly*, XVII, Spring, 1965.

Brockett, Linus P. *Woman's Work in the Civil War: A Record of Heroism, Patriotism and Patience*. Phila: Ziegler, McCurdy & Co., 1867.

Brooks, Van Wyck. *New England: Indian Summer, 1865-1915*. New York: E. P. Dutton & Co., 1940.

Brooks, Van Wyck. *The Flowering of New England, 1815-1865*. Cleveland, N.Y.: World Publishing, 1946.

Brown, Herbert Ross. *The Sentimental Novel in America, 1789-1860*. Chapel Hill: 1940.

Canby, Henry Seidel. *Thoreau*. Boston: Houghton Mifflin Co., 1939.

Carlyle, Thomas. *Sartor Resartus*. Boston, London: Athenaeum Press, 1896.

Carove, Friederich Wilhelm. *Story Without an End*, trans. Sarah Austin, preface by B. Alcott. Boston: Roberts Bros., 1848.

Clark, Annie M. L. *The Alcotts in Harvard*. Lancaster, Mass.: JCC Clark, 1902.

Claudy, Frank. *Goethe's Faust*, trans. Frank Claudy. Washington: William H. Morrison, 1886.

Commager, Henry Steele. *Theodore Parker: Yankee Crusader*. Boston: Beacon Press, 1962.

Conway, Jill. "Women Reformers and American Culture, 1870-1930." *Journal of Social History*, V, Winter, 1971-72.

Cott, Nancy. *Root of Bitterness, Documents of the Social History of American Women*. New York: E. P. Dutton, 1972.

Cunnington, C. Willett. *Feminine Attitudes in the Nineteenth Century.* London: William Heinemann, Ltd., 1935.

Davis, David Brion. *Homicide in American Fiction 1798-1860; A Study in Social Values.* Ithaca, N.Y.: Cornell Univ. Press, 1957.

Demos, John. "Developmental Perspectives on the History of Childhood." *The Journal of Interdisciplinary History*, II, Autumn, 1971.

Edgarton, S. C. "Female Culture." *Mother's Assistant*, III, April, 1843.

Emerson, Ralph Waldo. *Selections from Ralph Waldo Emerson*, ed. by Stephen E. Whicher. Boston: Houghton Mifflin, 1957.

Fiedler, Leslie A. *Love and Death in the American Novel.* New York: Stein & Day, 1966.

Flexner, Eleanor. *Century of Struggle.* New York: Atheneum, 1971.

Gaskell, Elizabeth. *The Life of Charlotte Brontë.* London: Smith, Elder & Co.; New York: Scribner, Welford, 1873.

Gowing, Clara. *The Alcotts As I Knew Them.* Boston: C. M. Clark, 1909.

Graves, A. J. *Woman in America.* New York: Harper & Bros., 1843.

Harris, Seale. *Woman's Surgeon, The Life History of J. Marion Sims.* New York: Macmillan, 1950.

Hoftadter, Beatrice K. "Popular Culture and the Romantic Heroine." *American Scholar*, XXX, Winter, 1960-61.

James, Henry. "Miss Alcott's Moods." *North American Review*, July, 1865; reprinted in *Henry James, Notes & Reviews*, Dunsterhouse, 1968.

Kett, Joseph F. "Adolescence and Youth in Nineteenth Century America." *The Journal of Interdisciplinary History*, II, Autumn, 1971.

Kraditor, Aileen. *Means and Ends in American Abolitionism.* New York: Pantheon Books, 1967.

Kuhn, Anne L. *The Mother's Role in Childhood Education: New England Concepts, 1830-1860.* New Haven: Yale Univ. Press, 1947.

Kyrd, Hazel. *The Family in the American Economy.* Chicago: University of Chicago Press, 1953.

Lee, Eliza Buckminster. *Life of Jean Paul Frederic Richter.* Boston: Ticknor and Fields, 1864.

Lerner, Gerda. "The Lady and the Mill Girl: Changes in the Status of Women in the Age of Jackson." *Midcontinent American Studies Journal,* X, (1969).

Lewis, R. W. B. *The American Adam / Innocence, Tragedy and Tradition in the Nineteenth Century.* Chicago: Univ. of Chicago Press, 1961.

Martineau, Harriet. *Society in America,* vols. 1 & 2. New York: Saunders & Otley, 1837.

Meigs, Cornelia. *Invincible Louisa.* Boston: Little, Brown & Co., 1933.

Miller, Perry. *Consciousness in Concord. The Text of Thoreau's Hitherto Lost Journal, 1840-1845 with Notes and Commentary.* Boston: Houghton Mifflin, 1958.

McCuskey, Dorothy. *Bronson Alcott, Teacher.* New York: The Macmillan Co., 1940.

O'Neill, William L. *Everyone Was Brave.* Chicago: Quadrangle Books, 1969.

Ossoli, Margaret Fuller. *Woman in the Nineteenth Century,* ed. by Arthur B. Fuller. Boston: Roberts Brothers, 1893.

Papashivily, Helen Waite. *All the Happy Endings, a Study of the Domestic Novel in America, the Women Who Wrote It, the Women Who Read It, in the Nineteenth Century.* New York: Harper & Bros., 1956.

Parker, Theodore. "The Public Function of Woman," reprinted in Theodore Parker, *Sins and Safeguards of Society.* Boston: American Unitarian Assoc., Vol. 9, 1907.

—— "On the Labouring Classes," reprinted in Theodore Parker, *Social Classes in a Republic.* Boston: American Unitarian Assoc., Vol. 10, 1907.

Porter, Maria S. *Recollections of Louisa May Alcott, John Greenleaf Whittier, Robert Browning.* Boston: New England Magazine Corporation, 1893.

Riegel, Robert. "Women's Clothes and Women's Rights." *American Quarterly*, XV, Fall, 1963.

——. *American Feminists.* Lawrence, Kan.: Univ. of Kansas Press, 1963.

Rothman, David J. "Documents in Search of a Historian: Toward a History of Children and Youth in America." *The Journal of Interdisciplinary History*, II, Autumn, 1971.

Sennett, Richard C. and Jonathan Cobb. *The Hidden Injuries of Class.* New York: Knopf, 1972. Reviewed by Murray Kempton, "Blue Collar Blues," *New York Review of Books*, Feb. 8, 1973.

Smith, Daniel Scott. "Family Limitation, Sexual Control and Domestic Feminism in Victorian America: Toward a History of the Average American Woman." Unpublished Paper.

Stern, Madeleine B. *Louisa May Alcott.* London: Peter Nevill Ltd., 1950.

Stone, Julius. *Human Law and Human Justice.* Stanford: Stanford Univ. Press, 1965.

Strickland, Charles. "A Transcendentalist Father: The Child Rearing Practices of Bronson Alcott." *Perspectives in American History*, III, 1969, Charles Warren Center for Studies in American History, Cambridge, Mass.

Strout, Cushing. *The American Image of the Old World.* New York: Harper & Row, 1963.

Swift, Jonathan. *A Tale of the Tub.* London: Geo. Bell & Sons, 1907.

Taylor, William R. and Christopher Lash. "Two 'Kindred Spirits': Sorority and Family in New England, 1839-1846." *New England Quarterly*, XXXVI, March, 1963.

Tharp, Louise Hall. *The Peabody Sisters of Salem.* Boston: Little, Brown & Company, 1950.

Thoreau, Henry David. *Miscellanies.* Boston: Houghton Mifflin, 1893.

51

———. *Friendship.* New York: Thomas Y. Crowell & Co., 1906.

Ticknor, Caroline. *May Alcott, A Memoir.* Boston: Little Brown & Co., 1927.

Wahr, Frederick B. *Emerson and Goethe.* Ann Arbor, Mich.: Geo. Wahr, 1915.

Wayman, Margaret. "The Rise of the Fallen Woman." *American Quarterly*, III, Summer, 1951.

Wells, Robert V. "Demographic Change and the Life Cycle of American Families." *The Journal of Interdisciplinary History*, II, Autumn, 1971.

Welter, Barbara. "The Cult of True Womanhood: 1820-1860." *American Quarterly*, XVIII, Summer, 1966.

Whicher, Stephen E. *Freedom and Fate, an Inner Life of Ralph Waldo Emerson.* Phila.: Univ. of Penn. Press, 1953.

Willis, Frederick L. H. *Alcott Memoirs.* Boston: Richard G. Badger, 1915.

Wood, Ann D. "The Scribbling Women and Fanny Fern: Why Women Wrote." *American Quarterly*, XXIII; Spring, 1971.

Woolf, Virginia. *Collected Essays*, Vol. 2. London: Hogarth Press, 1925.

Worthington, Marjorie. *Miss Alcott of Concord.* New York: Doubleday & Co., 1958.

Young, Agatha. *The Woman and the Crisis.* New York: McDowell, Obocensky, 1959.

CHAPTER I

A Pair of Friends

A tap at the studio door broke the silence which had lasted for hours, and the busy worker looked up with an impatient, "Who is there?"

"Only Percy."

"Come in! Come in!" and throwing down her tools the young woman in the linen pinafore hastened to greet the newcomer with a sudden kindling of the absorbed face which showed how welcome she was.

"You have come to tell me something!" she exclaimed, the moment her eye fell upon that other face, more than ever unlike her own, for an unusually resolute expression made it both brilliant and intense.

"Yes, I have decided at last," and Percy threw her hat into one chair, herself into another with a somewhat tragical air.

"You have said yes?"

"I have said no."

"Thank heaven for that!" and Diana shook hands with an animation which was as sure as becoming.

"I knew *you* would be satisfied if no one else was," said Percy smothering a sigh, for she had a right womanly heart and it always ached when she was forced to utter that hard monosyllable to one of her many lovers.

"I am *never* satisfied and never expect to be, with myself at least," and the keen clear eyes glanced round

53

the room as if seeking vainly for any touch of perfection in the plaster, iron and marble figures that stood there as beautiful and calm as herself.

"For that reason it is both good and bad for me to have you for a bosom friend. You spur me on and you discourage me at the same time; for I must walk only in one path—and if I look to the right or left you frown upon me. I've told you one decision that pleases you, now I'll tell another that will displease you, though you ought to approve it since it is the right way: I am going abroad," announced Percy with something of the rapture which is always visible in the faces of art lovers when uttering those joyful words.

"Again?" asked Diana in surprise.

"Again. The first time I went to wonder, admire and discover what a conceited ignoramus I was to call myself an artist. Now I am going to begin more humbly and work hard for two or three years at least, content to call myself a student, nothing more."

"Humility is a good sign, especially when one has much to be proud of. But can you leave your Grandmother?"

"If we give ourselves entirely to Art we must trample on Nature occasionally; so in escaping from the lovers who annoy me to the work I prefer I must also turn my back on the last of my kindred and my dearest friend. Unless she will come too?" and Percy opened her arms with a look and gesture which would have made a sympathetic observer pity the unfortunate lovers whom she was eluding.

But Diana shook her head decidedly.

"No, dear, it is impossible. My time has not come yet and I have much to do before I am ready. But I am glad *you* are going though it leaves me forlorn, for in giving yourself wholly to work you will escape the temptations that beset you here. Now tell me about it." As if the thought of approaching separation melted away the native coldness that lay like a light frost upon her youth and beauty, she sat down beside her friend with a face full of affectionate interest.

"I am tired of everything! Especially of waiting for inspiration; I cannot find it here so I am going to look for it," began Percy, leaning back with her hands clasped over her head in a posture full of graceful abandon and an expression of ardent discontent which betrayed a liberty loving nature trying to divine and obey instincts as unerring as the flower's love of light, the bird's impulse to sing.

" 'Genius is infinite patience,' you remember," and Diana pointed to the motto of Michael Angelo inscribed above her door.

"Genius makes its own mood, talent needs much help and gets discouraged if there's one too many obstacles to surmount."

"I'm afraid you will always have one sort of obstacle in your way because you cannot help being most attractive and loveable," said Diana, fondly smoothing the breezy brown locks which framed a face far less beautiful than her own but infinitely more lovely, being full of the color, light, and changefulness which makes a woman's countenance enchanting.

"Oh yes, I can! I intend to brush out my curls, wear that unbecoming sage green gown of mine and look as repulsively plain and artistically absorbed as possible," laughed Percy, holding back the rebellious waves that clustered about cheek and forehead as if they loved to keep touching these.

Diana smiled also but was not satisfied, for though the change added age, it also discovered the fine lines traced by five and twenty years of a very earnest life, making the face both sweet and noble.

"Unfortunately men have eyes all the world over and foreigners use them more freely than our courteous countrymen, so I shall still tremble for you, Percy."

"You need not, except in England. There I shall feel at home and maybe in danger. I so much admire color, strength and stature in both men and women. On the continent I will veil myself like a vestal virgin and keep the vow I make my chosen goddess, Diana."

"My vengeance will be heavy if you forget. But, seriously, are you bent on this, Percy, or is it only one of your impatient moods?"

"Seriously I am bent on this, and it is not a passing mood. I am impatient— because I feel power of some sort stirring in me, yet I cannot put it into any shape that satisfies me."

"It satisfies others and that is a great deal. How many women of your age have done so much, made so excellent a beginning, and won such genuine praise? Most people would be content to stop, for a time at least, to enjoy their success."

"I cannot! I have not *earned* my success, it came by accident. My work is not thoroughly good, only striking; for I aimed high and audacity always tells at first; but when the novelty of style wears off, the poverty of the material will show. I know I *can* do better if I can only get more criticism and less praise; find the right atmosphere, the right inspiration, and really do my best."

"And you hope to discover both in Rome?" asked Diana, looking as if the noble discontent of her friend woke some longings in her own ambitious soul.

"No, Rome will come later; Paris is the place to study in, and that is what I want (prefer). My eye for color is a gift that blinds me as well as others to my bad drawing, so I am going to sit on the low seats and learn.

A year of hard work at it will do me good, for those Frenchmen *can* draw, though their coloring is often atrocious. I know this is what I need and I mean to have it at any price. Here there are too many pleasures to distract me, too many temptations to let my art go and do as other women do. Grandmamma says I should be happier if I did. Perhaps she is right—I certainly need motive of some sort if only I knew where to find it." Percy's face seemed to sharpen with the keen anxiety of a nature both impetuous and conscientious, longing to find and do the right.

"Don't look for it in marriage, that is too costly an experiment for us. Flee from temptation and do not dream of spoiling your life by any commonplace romance, I implore you," cried Diana earnestly, and this was not the first time she had given the same advice.

"Yet love is the great teacher they say. I want to learn of the best. I am half tempted to try sometimes, for I have a hungry heart as well as an ambitious spirit and art alone does not seem to satisfy me as it does you."

There was a touch of pathos in the girl's voice and a wistful look in the eyes that wandered around the large, bare room, coldly lighted from the north and peopled with many forms, classic beauty; a strong contrast to the sunshine, life and warmth that filled her own little studio and made it as charming as herself.

"Percy, you regret that last no, and this new plan is a flight because you doubt yourself?" and Diana took the clouded face in her two hands to read it with scrutiny.

The frank eyes met her gaze freely though the sensitive lips trembled a little as they answered with a smile half proud, half sad.

"I regret nothing; but it is always hard to deny what most women delight to give and receive. If I had a marble heart like you, I should be much happier."

"You would lose your greatest charm which is your tender and sympathetic nature. You could not paint as you do without it, for warmth and color are your delight as clay and stone are mine, and we are both suited to our work."

Diana kissed the face and let it go reluctantly as if peculiarly conscious of the charm just then.

"That reminds me! I want your opinion of a little thing I have here; just a fancy; a thought rather," said Percy rising to untie the parcel she had thrown down with her hat.

Leaning it against the august knees of a Pallas on the bracket opposite, she resumed her seat and silently watched her friend as she examined it. Only an unframed canvas, high and narrow, with a mere suggestion of a grassy field below, all above was sky meeting from silvery morning mist through sunny blue to the palest gold, and midway between, a bird soaring and singing with open beak and head thrown back as if its Heaven's gate was the goal of its desire.

A simple thing, but exquisitely painted, for one seemed to feel the cool breath of early day, to see the little bosom swell and quiver with its ecstatic music, and following the lark's flight to echo the immortal songs that make it an emblem of aspiration.

"Percy, it is *very* good! The rising mist is wonderful and that sky simply perfect. I never saw a lark go up but I know how it looks. You were not waiting for inspiration when you did this for sure," said Diana with conviction, her eye still on the picture, giving it the commendation of perceptive interest which artists value more than words of praise.

"Glad you like it. I have a superstitious sort of feeling about it because it was born of a mood, and I sometimes find when I follow such that they lead me to unexpected results. I was very dismal and discontented the other day, longing for something fresh and cheery to lift me out of the fog, and suddenly I found myself recalling a certain summer morning when I lay under a yellow gorse bush on Wimbledon Common and saw the larks go up while talking about ambition with my friend Vaughn. I *was* waiting for inspiration; it came in this form, I fell to work, and when my picture was done I had decided to go ahead."

"For another talk about ambition under the gorse bushes?" asked Diana, with a suspicious glance and a sudden recollection of Percy's words, "No longer except in England."

"Vaughn's wife and pretty boys were with us, so you need not smile in that satiric way. I am done with lovers and leave them all behind me, I devoutly hope," answered Percy, with a disdainful shrug. "Would you like it better if the foreground were more clearly defined?" she added, going back to her picture as if the other subject had lost all interest for her. "Grandmamma said it tired her to think the poor lark had no place to rest in, (being a bird and not a spirit) because no bird that flies is without a nest of some sort, and sings the sweeter for it."

"Pretty sentiment, but the picture is better without it. Anyone can paint a nest but few a sky like that and make us feel in looking at the lark, 'Bird thou never wert.'"

"Thanks." Grandma admired it very much but said, "If you mean a spirit paint one, my dear, but if you want that bird to be happy give her a comfortable nest full of little responsibilities, for the highest flyers need a home and that lark for all its twittering has got to drop sometime since it cannot live in the clouds."

"You certainly have one frank criticism. Nevertheless I am glad you did not spoil your work. My lark does not stoop to fill gaping beaks with worms while her own is full of music that delights all ears, nor sit content among the daisies when she can fly above the clouds," said Diana, jealously covering with her slender hand the vague hint of a nest in the foreground.

"Yet the same instinct that sent her up brings her down, so I suppose she is wise to follow it, and Grandma may be right after all." And Percy stared thoughtfully at a dusty engraving of the Cotter's Saturday Night tucked behind the Minerva as of little worth.

"Follow the instinct that takes you away from all sickly sentiment before you disgrace yourself. When do you go?" asked Diana, returning abruptly to the safer topic.

"Next week. Solitary confinement and hard work for one year at least is my sentence, so you see I am to atone for my errors and be a credit to you. It will have an excellent effect upon me, I am sure, and tone me down till I am steadfast, calm and contented as my model. Art is a jealous mistress and now I give myself to her entirely."

Percy threw herself into the arms of her friend with a dramatic gesture, as if she personified the austere goddess henceforth to be served with perfect devotion.

"Now I am pleased with you and prophesy great things of you. Hold fast to your purpose and in a year or two I will come rejoice over you, and we will go to Rome together."

"We will!" and the friends sealed the bargain with a laughing embrace, both being heartily in earnest and both glad to sweeten the sorrow of separation by the thought of that happy reunion. "Now what can I do to help? If you sail in a week you leave yourself little time for preparation," said Diana, as Percy took up her hat.

"I need even less than I have because I leave all my finery behind me and go in light marching order as becomes a student who means work. I've nothing to do but buy a pea jacket, pack my paint box and a few old gowns, kiss Grandma and be off," answered Percy, assuming a brisk and breezy air pleasant to behold.

"You will write often, for I shall be so lonely and so interested in all you do I shall depend on long and frequent letters."

"That will be the one luxury I shall allow myself. But the letters will be dull, I warn you, for I shall keep out of society and have no gaiety to report. I intend to live like a hermit and toil like a slave, for it is possible to do both in dear delightful Paris, as many a hardworking student can tell you."

"Don't live alone. It is not good for a social girl like you, though it suits me excellently. Hunt up some of our old mates and make one of the busy little households we hear about over there. Now promise me you will?" and Diana anxiously urged her point, for the idea of this impulsive, attractive creature trying to live alone oppressed her as if she saw a child about to be shut into a prison cell.

"My dear soul, I'm going straight to Anna Becker and her cousin who have been there several years and are continually begging me to come and join them. That will be my refuge for a time, just while I look about me and settle my plans. The vastness and vagueness of the whole expedition is its charm. I feel like Columbus going to discover a new world, for when I went before, it was as a fine lady with all proper guards and guides; now I go alone with only my own common sense and courage to protect me."

"How did you ever bring your Grandmother to consent, and you the apple of her eye?" asked Diana looking with both wonder and admiration at this energetic friend of hers who, though some years her junior, was launching her little boat so bravely and blithely into the sea of experience and leaving so much behind her.

"The dear old lady is a wise woman who believes that we must each live out our own life in our own way and it is folly to try and shape us all in the same mould. She knows that I shall drift into matrimony with half a heart unless I break away and follow my heart till I am satisfied. So she lets me go with her blessing and not a word of complaint, like a Spartan mother as she is. A sacrifice for both of us, but she shall be proud of me and so I will repay her."

Percy's eyes shone eager, proud and tender through the sudden dew that rose to them and it was plain to see that her share of the sacrifice was not a light one.

"I know you will! And while you are gone I shall try to fill our place, and in rejoicing over you we shall comfort one another."

"I give you an order for a bust of her; it is too fine a head to be lost and in making it you will come to know and love one another better for my sake. Will you do this for me? Put the dear old face in marble since it cannot be immortal otherwise, and I may not find it here when I come back," added Percy with a sudden falter in her voice that made refusal impossible.

"I will, and put my heart into the work. It is so like you to do a kindness as if receiving a favor! You shall pay for the bust in letters; I will take no other coin," and Diana put both hands on her friend's shoulders to enforce her words with the gentle pride which no poverty could humble since affection and principle ennobled it.

"As you like; and I'll send you my first great picture in return," began Percy, privately resolving to circumvent her friend in some way.

"No, leave me this unless you value it too much," interrupted Diana, taking up the little canvas with a face full of fond covetousness. "Your Grandmother will not care for it since it tires her. I like it; I too have a superstitious feeling about it, and associate it with you, fancying I can watch your flight as I watch this bird with its spread wings and open beak just passing out of the mist into the blue above."

"Keep it then until I send a letter, showing that ambitious fowl high up against the gold." For a moment the two stood looking silently at the dumb canvas which was as eloquent to their eyes as a cloud of stirring music to a musician's ear, a key to the great symphony which in tone or color, thought or deed makes life harmonious for earnest livers.

"Now I must go. Come tomorrow and help me choose the pea jacket. I can't fly off so easily as the swallows on their journey south, more's the pity," said Percy, descending suddenly into the commonplace as a relief from too much feeling.

"Good bye, my lark, soar and sing and get above the clouds as soon as possible, and stay there as long as you can," answered Diana, with a gaiety that thinly veiled more serious significance.

"Good bye, my eagle; however high I go I shall find you before me, for you can look at the sun with unwinking eyes and your wings never tire; while I can only twitter up a little way and tumble down again all out of breath," answered Percy with equal meaning and went away humming to herself.

Higher still and higher
From the earth thou springest
Like a cloud of fire;

The deep blue thou wingest,
And singing still dost soar,
And soaring ever singest.

These two had been friends from girlhood, the tie between them being artistic ambition and a sincere respect for each other's powers. Both were unusually gifted, not only with talent but with the courage and patience which are the wings of genius; and after ten years of steady upward climbing they were now ready for the flight out of the world of effort into the region of achievement, that promised land which so many sigh for and never see.

Diana stood alone now, a strong, self-reliant woman of twenty-eight; looking always with calm persistence at the purpose of her life, to reach Rome and there do the great work which should unlock the golden future to her longing soul. No nun in her cell ever led a more austere and secluded life than this fine creature intent upon her self-appointed task.

Denying herself the pleasures of youth, the honors of sex and beauty, the joys of love, the solaces of home, she went on her steadfast way, unresting and unhasting as a star; as cold and brilliant and remote to all except the few who had discovered hidden fires in this fair planet. Bread and the right to work was all she asked of the world as yet. One friendship was the only luxury she allowed herself and in this she found not only the solace but the stimulant she needed, for it was a most sincere and sympathetic bond.

Percy had blossomed in a sunnier soil and from it gathered the warm, rich nature which makes some women among their kind what roses are among the flowers, thorny yet sweet, infinitely various but always lovely and beloved. A happy childhood, a free, fresh girlhood, and now a womanhood full of promise, because the wise and earnest culture of those years began to blossom into high thoughts, courageous action, noble purposes, which time alone could ripen.

What adversity had done for Diana, prosperity had done for Percy and each drew from the soil of life the nourishment she needed, growing toward the sun of their desire slowly and steadily as green things struggle up in spring. The same aim was theirs, success and happiness; but with Diana success came first, with Percy happiness; both being conscious at times of that secret warfare of thwarted instincts and imperious ambitions, the demands of temperament as well as of talent, the lessons Nature teaches all of us in ways more mysterious and masterful than any one can give.

Diana was the stronger willed woman, Percy the deeper hearted, and each found in the other the attributes most needed to complete her own character. Not a sentimental but a most helpful and enduring affection which had lasted unbroken for years and might still live for many more unless the master passion which dissolves all lesser ties should come between them. As yet it had not, for Diana hid herself in her little studio, consecrating even her beauty to her art, and being her own model, since a better it would be hard to find, and Percy staunchly tried to follow her example in spite of many obstacles, her winsome self included.

That genial old gentlewoman Madam Lennox made a most attractive home for her granddaughter in whom was bound up her love and hope and pride, for she was the last of her line. Wisely leaving the girl to unfold as God willed, the tender soul hid her own doubts and desires, waiting for time to teach and love to tame the ardent, ambitious girl.

Percy could no more help having lovers than a clover can forbid the bees and butterflies from coming for its honey, and but for her dreams of art, she might soon have found her fate as many a young girl does, believing that women were born to be wives only, and finding out too late that every soul has its own life to live and cannot hastily ignore its duties to itself without bitter suffering and loss. Fortune she had not, being dependent on her kinswoman, but youth and the gift of attraction, more potent than beauty, she had in fullest measure, and the cordial grace of her frank manners, the enthusiasm which went into everything she did, the quick sympathy that was a key to all natures, made her a very winning woman, and there was no lack of suitors for so loyal a heart, so generous a hand.

But Percy's ideal was a high one, and with the arrogance of happy youth she would abate no item in the list of virtues which made up the perfect man who was her hero, so the enamoured gentlemen pleaded all in vain. Diana, devoutly believing that "Success is impossible, unless the passion for art overcomes all desultory passions," held Percy to her ideal with stern vigor, always hoping that the time would come when her friend would give all to art and let love go, as she herself had done. Therefore she trembled at every temptation, rejoiced at every fresh denial, and now although her heart sunk at the thought of its great loneliness in losing Percy, she bade her go, sure that in work alone her salvation as an artist lay.

Hiding her pain with a heroic smile, she went to say farewell when the last hour came, and Percy, equally heavy hearted but not equally strong, clung to her with the remorseful tenderness of those who go toward those left behind. Both kept up bravely till the great steamer swung round into the stream, then both hearts swelled to overflowing and tears dimmed the eyes that sought and held each other across the widening gulf between them.

"In a year!" cried Percy, leaning down for one last hopeful word.

"Remember!" answered Diana, with a warning gesture toward the nosegay in her friend's hand, a farewell taken from the lover who dared not come to reutter what the roses sweetly said for him.

"I will!" and with a tearful laugh, an impulsive motion, Percy flung the poor flowers far away into the bitter waves that swept them out of sight among the foam.

Diana waved her hand, well pleased at this brave casting behind her of all dangerous sentiment, and dashing the rare drops from her own eyes watched till the receding figure could be no longer seen, then turned away, thinking with a desolate sort of resignation—"My work still remains, and that must satisfy me, for a year at least."

But Percy went below to hide her tears, saying with a sob in her throat as she tenderly removed a little spray of green which had blown back and clung to the rough bosom of her pea-coat when she flung away the nosegay.

("I'm glad to keep one token of the dear mother earth to comfort me when I am all alone on the great cold sea.")

"Love won't be disowned, it seems; I'll keep this bit of sentiment to comfort me when I'm homesick all alone on the great, cold sea."

CHAPTER II

Letters

Sept.

"Dearest Di.

My first letter telling of my voyage and safe arrival was to Grandmamma of course, but this shall be all yours, for in it I will unfold my projects and tell you how propitious the fates have been.

Straight to Paris and Anna Becket did I come, for London in the autumn does not tempt me, though I did take a peep at my beloved National Gallery the one day I passed there. I found Anna and her cousin Cordelia settled in a nice little apartment at the foot of Montmartre, with its picturesque old windmill to gladden our eyes when we look out from our sixth story windows, for like true artists we live up among the clouds. Not a fashionable but an eminently respectable Quarter, I beg to assure you, for Thiers lives just around the corner as it were. Three tiny bedrooms, a pretty salon, and studio with a kitchen is our establishment and here we live, the merry spinsters, doing most everything for ourselves in the simple, free and easy way best suited to our professions and our purses.

My friends are capital girls and welcomed me so kindly that I felt at home at once, and thanked my fortunate stars that I had found so pleasant a refuge and such congenial comrades. By Anna's advice I

69

went immediately to K's studio for women and entered my name as a pupil; for it gives us most of the advantages of J's great school for men and women. We pay more but we are spared many of the trials which afflict us at the other place. We looked in at J's where most of the great painters have studied till they went to the Beaux Arts, and here we found a fine model posing to a crowd of men who whistled, sang and joked while drawing away in the most vigorous style. I could not have borne it if there had been no other place for us, but felt very grateful that there was. At K's I find a good earnest set of women and our master is a most agreeable man and a fine teacher. Three of the best painters in France come twice a week to criticize and correct our work. There are fourteen pupils, in the morning, all American or English and as many more in the afternoon, but a younger set. By paying for both classes one can also draw in the evening as gaslight is considered excellent for the shadows.

I see that it will be best for me to work all day for six months at least, drawing the ensemble in the morning and painting in oils from the head only in the afternoon. I shall not try work in the evening as I need the rest and time to do other things. Working from life models is most exciting as you know, but, Di, *we* never had such grand ones as these, and I long for you every time I sit down before one of them.

Our model this week is Italian with a superb physique and the head of a god. His rich coloring distracts me because I can not paint it all day, and I try vainly to get a good copy of his great dark eyes, proudly dilating nostrils and picturesque head with its jovelike curls. The pose is perfect, and it is wonderful how he can keep it so long. Figure to yourself the difficulty; head thrown back, eyes raised, stepping forward with an air of rapid motion in every limb, and so he stands for an hour like a statue, and we draw like mad, for soon great drops come upon his forehead and every muscle shows, so great the effort and yet so perfect his control. He has been a model for years and is so proud of his posing that his indignation knew no bounds when one of the ladies suggested that he was not quite in position. With a glance of scorn he threw himself into a magnificent pose and did not deign us any further notice that session.

So much for school, which I find intensely interesting and work with all my soul, as it is impossible to help doing here, for nothing draws me away as at home and I never tire though I never toiled so hard. You may like a sketch of our day, uneventful as it usually is. We are up early, daylight being precious and in our wrappers, "fly round" each doing her share, for thus is housekeeping made easy. One steps into the little kitchen and puts a match to the few bits of charcoal needed to make our coffee or chocolate, another dusts the salon and studio, the third runs out to do our daily marketing and order dinner from the restaurant nearby. We take our coffee and rolls while dressing, talking and laughing all together, in the jolliest way. Isn't Grandma shocked? Then Anna makes ready for her sitters (she is a portrait painter, you know, and does wonders in that line). Cordy retires to her den to write the letters you must read in the American papers, and I hurry away to school, eager to be at work though I hate drawing in black and white and long for my colors. At twelve I run home for a hot breakfast, or lunch we should call it, cooked by the girls who make the most delicious messes out of nothing in the true French style. Then back to work till dusk which always comes too soon for me. We dine at six and in the evening sew, study, see friends and frolic in a mild antic manner, going to bed early to sleep well and dream of immortality.

I told you my letters would be dull and you see how quiet life is likely to be. But I did not come to play and I am more than ever convinced that this is the best place in the world to study, though it takes the conceit out of one to see how these people work. Careful drawing from the life model to begin with, whether landscape or figure is to be the profession afterward; the same routine that Broyan, Dupais and Casant went through for years before their reputations were established. It must be hard study for a year or so at least and no "pot boilers" allowed, to help out expenses. But they are very smart living in the cozy, simple way we do, and six or seven hundred a year is enough for women who take no thought for frippery and frivolity. A thousand is a fortune, so, thanks to the dearest old lady in the world, I am quite a millionaire.

Only here a fortnight and I already begin to dream of the Salon which alone makes a name for the happy soul who gets in. There's audacity for you! I always did aim high, and in two years I will be far up the tree with every prospect of a perch in the topmost twig in time. It is impossible to help being sanguine and ambitious, for the earnestness I find here is most contagious and one cannot take hold of painting superficially when everybody is intent on doing his or her very best. Art pervades the air, everyone paints, all the talk is of pictures, color. Shapes surround us, studios are thicker than houses in this quarter, and at 8 a.m. the streets swarm with artists of all nationalities, paint box in hand, hurrying in every direction with absorbed faces. I am told there are forty thousand of these ambitious souls in France alone, all trying to go where glory awaits them, and Paris seems to be their headquarters; so you cannot wonder that the fever rages here and I am rapidly falling a victim to it, being a susceptible creature as you know.

Now, dear, I have told you my debut, so don't imagine me gamboling about this gay city with wild students, or leading a Bohemian life while pretending to study. Think of me always as in deadly earnest, for this is the place to meet one's fate, success or failure, and I am started on the exciting race, so wish me God speed, and write often to keep me up to the mark as you always can.

A thousand loves to dear Grandma. My next shall be to her, for you must take turns and so will get variety.

Ever yours,
p.l."

Nov.

"Dear Di.

All the gossip I could collect went to Grandmamma last week, so I can drop into Art for you this time, having nothing else to offer. It is Sunday, and after going to church like good girls, we sit in our little salon round the first fire of the season painting while Cordy reads aloud, for without a brush or crayon in our hands we feel like old ladies bereft of their knitting. I am at work on a still life study just for practice. A brass brazier standing on a dark polished table with a scarlet flower in it. Anna is putting the last touches to a splendid portrait of a handsome lady in black velvet, sitting on a yellow satin sofa, gorgeous to behold. Cordy is reading the newspaper letter of a Paris correspondent which she means to answer as we are all indignant about it. It is just such hastily written, one-sided things that do infinite harm at home by prejudicing people against aiding women in the art studies which they so much need; the obstacles being

73

so great that only those desperately earnest are able to surmount them at great cost of money, time and feeling. We should have had no fine pictures by Rosa Bonheur if with her tastes she had contented herself with flowers or still life, "the only things this writer considers delicate and proper for a lady's brush."

As for "the women who unsex themselves by going to J's studio," where alone they could get the teaching they needed, we think it a thing to heartily respect them for, as one respects those who study anatomy in order to be surgeons. That little band of dignified and earnest women so far from unsexing themselves were treated with the utmost respect at J's, and very soon made by their mere presence a purer atmosphere about them. Courage is honored everywhere, and this terrible effort to get the same advantages as men in the same profession at any cost, won for them a place at once in the regard of all real art students. I had rather the French judged us by these brave, rightminded women than by the frivolous creatures who bring discredit on the name of American girls by their wild pranks and empty heads.

We are twitted with getting no medals at the Salon. How can we when hitherto we were not allowed to study at the life schools yet expected to do as well in a third of the time and with half the help men have? How few of them get prizes with all their chances. Wait a little, Messieurs, give us a few years of equal teaching, equal opportunities and see what we will do.

Now I feel better and will go on more calmly and only I beg you will read my protest to all our mates and tell them not to be daunted but to come on, and do their best for every success helps us up.

I have little to report at the studio for it has been a steady grind for me, yet I like it and get on, I am sure. The great M, our most dreaded critic, when our studies were given to him to examine the other day asked, "Who did that?" and lo, it was mine. He gave me a look, a nod said, "This flesh is luminous," and looked again at my work, a head in oils. No more, but I was much elated and my mates patted me on the head when we were alone. I tell you this as my first small success, for you will understand how it cheers one after weeks of dogged work and the despondency that will come to the most sanguine of us when thinking how endless is the lesson we artists have to learn.

We have been a little gay this last week, and as I have made a new friend I will tell you of her, for she is one after your own heart. Miss Cassal comes to the studio to draw when we have a fine model and I liked her strong face the first time I saw it. She liked my work and came very kindly to tell me so one day when I was struggling with a hard lesson, for K would have me draw to the waist when I preferred only the head of our model. She asked me to come and see her and I went. She is a grand woman, full of real genius, I think, and but for her sex would have made a name before now, since all who know her acknowledge her power. She has the modesty of true talent and so is content to do fine things and let others get praised for mediocre work, she biding her time. Her pictures are handled in a masterly way and with a strength one seldom finds in a woman's fingers. I am told that men are jealous of her, and her "Joel" was refused at the last Salon merely because of its boldness and power. She smiles and paints on tranquilly, content to be felt if not seen. She has money and uses it nobly, not only in helping herself but others, and we have a plan in our heads to get up a school for women here as Rosa Bonheur did for girls under twenty; a studio where we can club together and have the best models and masters and a chance to show what we can do with a clear track and judges. Her enthusiasm delights me and we shook hands like old friends after my long visit full of the most interesting talk.

This week we went to tea in her studio which is a charming place and the resort of many of the young artists, men as well as women; there last evening, we met fifteen or twenty of them and had a most enjoyable time sitting in antique chairs on Persian rugs with tapestry backgrounds, fine pictures on the walls, pretty things all about us, and the whole lighted by hanging lamps in the most artistic and effective manner. Some of the men sang and we sipped tea and ate ice, but the talk was the best, for it was art, still art. I was much interested in several of these people and in answering my questions Miss C told me some pretty little stories about them, which you will like as they show how kind these artists are to one another.

One young man, an American, shy, awkward and plain but with an eye that is full of fire and a resolute mouth, was the hero of one tale. He has been plugging along here for some years on almost nothing, slowly but surely overcoming poverty, ignorance and neglect and at last begins to see light, having done a good picture and received an order or two (thanks to Miss C, I suspect). He was just rejoicing over his luck when he hurt his right hand seriously and could not work for some time. He was in despair, for he earns his daily bread with this right hand of his, but his friends came to the rescue and, knowing he was too proud to accept alms, asked him to be their model, as he has a fine stalwart figure. So he stands to them and is well paid, for they not only paint him but cheer him with friendly talk and a little kindness instead of leaving him to eat his heart out alone. "Now I like that!" says dear Grandmamma. So do I.

Here is another. A portrait painter, a woman (not Anna, she has more than she can manage, thank

Heaven!), wanted sitters but was unknown and too poor to fit up an attractive studio. A brother artist, with a name, offered to sit, knowing that she only needed a start to be appreciated. His portrait is a success; is exhibited in his own much frequented atelier and greatly admired; a good word is said for the painter and orders flow in. So the modest girl is led to the place she has earned by the kind hand of a comrade and puts all her heart into her work that she may prove her gratitude by being an honor to him.

These and many more like them did Miss C tell me, for she is a sort of refuge to the younger set, being forty and full of maternal sympathy and generosity which is so winning I don't wonder the poor fellows are glad to come to her with their hopes and plans, trials and defeats, and it is half comical and pathetic to hear about them.

We have our little society at home, for Anna and Cordy have a most interesting circle of friends, and in the evening they drop in to report progress and see how we are getting on. Our countrymen mostly, studying for dear life as we are, so our interests are the same and we can help one another in many ways. The little homes we women naturally make for ourselves are very attractive to these poor fellows, often homesick and lonely, longing for society after the day's work is done, and too poor or too wise to seek the sort easiest found in Paris. We can give them an innocent helpful kind of pleasure for which they are grateful, and they bring into our quiet lives the masculine element which stimulates us without harm, for we are all too busy for sentiment and are just good comrades, nothing more I assure you.

Clothes, my dear? In answer to your question regarding that usually all absorbing topic, I reply that I don't think of it. In fact, drawing such noble nude figures all day makes modern drapery seem impertinent and ugly and I long to dress with unique simplicity in a tunic and veil. The sage green serge is all I need for school, and the old wine-colored silk does well for evening when we receive. Indeed it is a success to my great amusement and I am glad I brought it to please Grandma, for Anna declares she will paint my portrait in it on the famous yellow sofa which comes into play continually. The effect will be Turneresque, and when it is done I'll send it to you labelled, "The Fighting Seinereraise," or a "Symphony in Red and Yellow," a la Whistler. No, Di, no new raiment even here in the Vanity Fair of the world. I want all my money for lessons and every hour of the time taken from dear Gran shall be spent in good honest work, not fun and feathers, for I mean to prove that some women do love art better than dress.

With which beautiful moral sentiment I will say adieu.

Ever your P."

Dec.

"*My Dear,*

I have neglected you shamefully of late, but I am so busy I really get only time for a hasty letter once a fortnight and my last two or three have been hardly worth sending. Work goes on apace, but the last week nothing interesting broke the daily routine, then the holy days were celebrated by two exciting events, for me at least. I have come to honor unexpectedly, and I must tell you about it like a vain peacock as I am. I was in the depths of discouragement on Monday and went to the Studio resolving to give it all up and sail in the next steamer. You know the state of mind, so I need not describe it. I found a new model, and sat down before him in despair for he was a grand figure and I felt that I was not in the mood to grapple with him.

The lesson was a full length drawing of this Othello, as I at once named the handsome Moor, who was really a chief in his own country, has been decorated for bravery in the Crimean War, and is now a famous model here in Paris.

If I could have put the fine dark face and red drapery into color I should have been happy, but as it was only drawing I did not get on very well till a discussion arose about the man. Two of the class are Southerners and were rather scornful about the "negro" as they called him. He could understand little English but I know he felt what was said, for his eye kindled and the brave breast with the scars on it (better than medals in my eyes), heaved now and then as if he longed to speak, while he looked what he is, every inch a soldier and a prince. I could not bear to have things said even in jest which might wound him since he could not [but] resent them, and getting excited by the discussion I gave an antislavery lecture which would have delighted Grandma, who longs for the stirring times when she and her stout-hearted contemporaries sat out many a mob knitting with majestic composure up aloft while brick bats and hard words flew about below.

Well I fired all my big guns and silenced the enemy after a lively skirmish, for we all took sides as K was in his room with the great M. So busy was I defending my man that I drew without thinking what I was about and when the time was up was surprised to see how well I had wrought both spirited pose and expression. We did not dream that the gentlemen heard or understood us, but when M came out to look at our work we discovered that he at least had. When he reached that dashing haphazard sketch of mine, he gave a decided nod which makes our hearts leap, and said as he looked carefully at it, "With what passion and enthusiasm you draw this ensemble! It is very vigorous; it shows your knowledge, not your scorn of the race. Mademoiselle, I make you my compliment," and with a bow he marched away.

He spoke in French. Othello understood and flashed a smile at me as he vanished behind the screen, leaving me as red, with surprise and pleasure, as the drapery he flung over his shoulder with a superb gesture.

Then did I vaingloriously exalt myself and strut gaily home to recount my triumph. Really, Di, it *was* well done, and I feel as if I had got a good grip at last, for what was very hard three months ago now grows more easy with each day's effort and now and then I seem to take a leap ahead. I am to paint my Prince soon, I will send him home if I do well, for I want you to see this fine head. Tell Grandma I owe this success to her, for the principles she taught me inspired my pencil and so brought me to honor.

On the spur of the moment I proposed that we present M with a grand bouquet on New Year's Day and the vote was unanimously carried. We have had a little Christmas merry-making and I, going at one skip from the Slough of Despond to my present high state of spirits, enjoyed the fun with all my heart. Durant, our friend who is sitting for Anna in cavalier costume, as I told you in my last, is a jolly soul and always doing kind things; so on Christmas Day among other gifts from other comrades came a great Christmas pie from him, for he lives like a luxurious bachelor in his own apartment with a first class cook.

A truly noble pie was this, with his crest in the crust and a great red rose was laid atop with a French air. We feasted on this delectable pastry and a turkey cooked in our own oven which with difficulty contained his grand proportions. A merry dinner, though we drank "to the absent" with full eyes and talked much of home. In the eve we sent back D's dish full of bonbons and a note of thanks illustrated by Anna. Our chosen bird, the owl, was drawn sitting on the back of a chair with a lace handkerchief at her eyes, and great tears dropping into an empty dish on the table below, while from her beak came the mournful strain, "Joys we have tasted."

Jan. 2nd
(4th)

"I left my letter open to add how nicely our little presentation went off. M was both surprised and pleased when our lovely great nosegay was presented, accompanied by a few grateful words. With the grace and address of a Frenchman, he paid us a pretty compliment by likening us to the flowers, as he thanked us for the honor we did him in giving him our photographs on New Year's Day. So now we all feel very friendly and begin the year in the best of spirits. I am disappointed at not having my Prince to paint at once, but he is elsewhere and I must wait. Meantime, with artistic versatility I go from heads to heels, for our model this week has not an interesting face so I take his legs, which are good. He wears leather breeches, worsted gaiters with tassels, and muddy shoes, as the rest only use his shaggy head. He naturally crossed these legs as he sat and I booked them, to the great amusement of the class, for they were done *con amore*, with big brushes and lots of paint, and do look as if they would get up and walk out of the canvas. K laughed when he saw it, but said, "That is good strong work," so I was satisfied and had a heavenly time daubing away with my "beloved paintpots" as Grandma and you irreverently call them. She would be scandalized at the state of my elbows, for I cannot

81

spare time to darn, so go in rags, "picturesque but not tidy," as she used to say when I went about professionally dishevelled. Yes, I do long for home, but must stay my time out, for I begin to feel as if I had the *right* to be here since I am really getting on, unless my master and mates deceive me. So you must prepare to join me in the autumn, and persuade the dear old lady to come along. You would find yourself a new world, and she would enjoy this life immensely. Tell her to remember how Mrs. G gallantly swung her bonnet on the Cheaps at seventy-five and so I do likewise. Come, oh come to

Your P."

March

"Oh my dearest Di, we live in such exciting times just now! I hardly know where to begin to tell about them. It is such a sudden plunge out of the last two or three months of dull grind into all sorts of hopes and plans and possible glories. You remember my despair over the failure of my Prince's head, and how I took to still life studies in a rage? Well, things never go as one expects and art is a continual surprise party. I did a stupid little affair one day; a bottle, jug and dish of fruit just as they happened to stand on our dining table with the oak wainscot for background. Anna praised it, but I, still smarting with my disappointment over the head, rather scoffed at it, calling it the "onions and copper kettle style," which I don't care for though it *is* good practice, I admit. I took it to school to be criticized and you may judge my astonishment when M came round to look at my drawing, and dismissing it with a word, took up the study which I had forgotten, saying (hold on to something, Di, for I am about to knock you down, metaphorically speaking) "Ha, this is excellent, I could not do better myself. Send it to the

82

Salon and I shall be proud to call you my *élève*." K stood by beaming upon me much pleased at the Master's praise, and before I could get my breath to reply, M said "Take that into the class and show those ladies what painting simply what you see without trying to *make a picture* will do for one, even without great practice." Then he looked again and repeated, *"Tres Bien, tres bien, Mademoiselle*; you cannot do better than to go on in this way. Send that to the Salon."

With this astonishing advice he left me, and I am hardly recovered from the agreeable shock yet. A more amazed young woman did not exist than I, and you will believe that my wits are quite gone when I tell you that I am actually going to send that insignificant study to the Salon. I shall never believe it is good till I see it there, for in spite of all my master says I feel that if I ever do win fame it will be in painting heads and not pots and pans. Mark my prophetic words, uttered this day from the tripod of a shabby music stool, for I am in an uplifted state and feel oracular.

Anna is going to send her portrait of me if she can get it done in time. It is capital, and I have put my study into a cheap frame, and mean to send it along as the most stupendous joke of the season. If it *is* accepted (which I don't dream of) it will be a great honor as I am but a beginner, and a fine feather in my cap. If I am refused (which I fully expect) it will be no disgrace as I am a foreigner, a woman without a name, and six thousand were refused last year.

Everyone is in a frenzy now, for next Monday the 18th is the day for sending in the pictures and I have caught the fever since all the artists are hurrying madly to get done. As my great work is finished, I sit every day to Anna, who has had other things on hand and so let my portrait lie by; but it does not need much time to finish it if the light will only be good. Did I tell you that we gave up the red dress, and I am in peacock blue with all my curls out on a holy day and a muff and a hat, which turn the studious grub into a gay butterfly! It is a good likeness and I shall send it to Grandma who will value it whether it is accepted or not. I am wanted and must fly, for I write with all my borrowed gauds on while waiting for Anna to snatch her dinner.

Later

Such a scramble! but it is over now, and I can tell of it, for it was splendid fun. For the last two or three days Anna has been painting at a great pace, and I have hardly stirred except to eat a morsel and get what sleep I could. Miss Carol came to help us along and we had gay suppers after the day's hurry was over. You would have laughed to see me rushing about in my swishing blue train and dashing hat while Anna tyrannized over me and Cordy brought us food, and friends kept dashing in to hear how we got on.

We finished in time and I was whisked into a fine frame and left to dry as fast as I could in a warm room till the man came for *both* our works. Glad to escape Miss C and I went off to see the pictures arrive at the *Palais de le Industrie* where an immense crowd was assembled; mostly art students who, as the pictures were carried up the steps and dumped to be registered, sent up howls of derision or cries of admiration at the work of anyone known to them.

It was intensely exciting, and we stood with a group of friends as anxious as ourselves; for as six o'clock drew near and wagon after wagon drove up to be unloaded, the painters got perfectly distracted and rushed the pictures up in desperate haste, the elegant frames flying in splinters sometimes, amid the jeers of the crowd and the groans of the poor artist who saw his treasured work thus sadly handled. We stood for three mortal hours and forgot weariness in our interest. Still our pictures did not arrive, and we set off down the long line of wagons to see if we could find them. Just driving up the last of six still waiting to be unloaded came our cart and Dumont hurried the men and out I came with my little study in its ten franc frame behind me. How we laughed as the pair were borne away to get in as they could, and did, thanks to D for the doors close at a certain hour and the judges are *inexorable*, so latecomers are lost.

(Being too excited to rest we went to the theatre and saw Paul and Virginia Channing played.) Then we went home (exhausted) and fell into our beds exhausted. Now we wait to know our fate. I am prepared for mine since I am sure the poor thing won't get in.

Your P"

April 11

"Hurrah! wave your hats and reward the little grey postman who brings the good news from Ghent to Aix. My picture is accepted! Yes, truly! at the great Salon where of 8,500 works sent in only 2,000 were accepted, and my small study was thought worthy of a place among them! I don't believe it, and I know you won't either; but I am going to see it hung among the rest and then I shall be able to grasp the amazing fact. Now aren't you glad you let me come, my dearest Grandma? Don't you rejoice over your wilful P, Diana? Wasn't I wise to follow my instinct and go where glory waited me? I must soberly confess that I do not in the least understand why that ordinary little thing got in; but being in I will try to treat it with due respect and not mourn over the splendid heads that I tried to finish and couldn't.

85

My lucky star is certainly in the ascendant this year, for Anna's portrait is also accepted and you should have seen the joyful festival we had the day the glad news came. Everyone congratulated us, and it was beautiful to see the rejoicing over the successful ones among us, the sincere sympathy felt for those who failed, as of course many did. If you two could only be here to share all this pleasure with me on the spot, I should be too happy. My pass permits me to go as often as I like and take my friends, so I long for Grandma to see a certain lady in blue sitting in state to be surveyed by admiring nations, and Di to behold how small a candle makes a great light in this naughty world.

On Varnishing Day I went early, and there in the first salon stood face to face with my study, which looked very like a postage stamp, surrounded by the immense pictures whose gilded frames seemed to make a sort of glory, to my eyes at least, about this unpretending child of mine. I looked at it with new respect and saw that it *was* good, vigorous work; simple in subject and unaffectedly treated. I fancy this very simplicity is the secret of its success, for we too often attempt more than we are equal to, and so fail. It is a good lesson to me and teaches me both humility and a proper regard for patient thoroughness rather than effective haste.

Not only do its neighbors give it dignity but the hanging committee did me the honor to put it so low as to be nearly on the line, a place artists often pay large bribes to the hangers to secure for their pictures. When I saw what fine specimens of still life are there, I was more than ever surprised that mine was accepted, for I have no friend at court and M. is not among the judges. So I had another private jubilee as I stood before my old blue jug and the straw-covered wine bottle, then, after reading my name in the fat catalogue with a nice little notice after it, I went on to view thirty more rooms full of pictures, feeling that I too was an artist!

As soon as our works are restored to our proud arms, I will bundle them home to you, for I quite ache to have you see them both. Now I can fall to work again with a brave heart, for I mean to do great things this year, and have a superior head in the next Salon. You know there is nothing so successful as success.

Yours ever P."

CHAPTER III

Puck

One February afternoon Diana went to the Pincio to watch the sunset, see her fellow creatures, and enjoy the ever new surprise of spring, coming so early, and with such a wealth of beauty here. All the world was there as usual; the band playing deliciously, the sky a blaze of gold and purple, and the air full of a soft stir, not only of human enjoyment but the more delicate life of awakening Nature. Contenting herself with a passing glance at the gay throng, the circling train of brilliant equipages, and the picturesque figures continually crossing her path, Diana glided away to the quieter recesses of the Pincio, where distance lent enchantment to the sweet clamor of the music, and softened the blended colors to hues as fine as those in the blooming terraces below.

Leaning on the low parapet, she refreshed her weary eyes by looking down into the Borghese Gardens with their avenues, stone pines "like green islands in the air," dancing fountains and ruined altars whence seemed to rise, like incense, the rich breath of hidden violets. In the blue distance shone Soracte clear against the sky; the dome of St. Peter's soared like a golden bubble above the city bathed in rosy light and from the campanelli came the chime of bells ringing the Ave Maria.

The tender mood that comes to most of us in such hours was upon Diana then, full of a pleasant weariness, of voiceless longings, and vague sweet expectations stirring softly like imprisoned butterflies when spring sunshine call them from the chrysalis. She thought of Percy, feeling solitary now her day's work was done, and tenderly imagined her happy in the nest that filled so fast the mother bird had little time for friendship. The thought of her own life, so high and lonely (with its many satisfactions), its ever growing ambition, and the sense of power that strengthened every year. Yet at times she was conscious of a deeper want, an unconquerable yearning, a bittersweet regret for something lost or never found; as if a timid [hand] was put forth and meeting no responsive grasp withdrew again into the soft gloom which wrapt that recess of her heart, even from herself.

As this rare emotion came and lingered for a moment, a sudden mist passed before her eyes, eyes grown spiritual with much gazing at fair ideals, but all the lovelier for the unwanted dew that softened their clear brightness. "I am homesick," she said smiling at herself, unconscious that she spoke aloud. "So am I," replied a child's voice and a small hand slipped into hers as it hung beside her. She turned quickly to find a little creature looking up at her with a pathetic expression in its lovely face. "A golden boy," as the Germans would have called him for he seemed made up of sunshine, so profuse was the bright hair that lay upon the shoulders and met a sort of glory about the head. A round and rosy face, eyes like violets, and a red mouth shaped for kissing gave one the impression of a cherub; but the frill of rich lace, encircling the throat like the cloud which often finishes off these bodiless babies, was in this case supplemented by a velvet tunic, and ended in a pair of sturdy legs, brave purple hose and two muddy little shoes, making up a very winsome mortal child of five or six.

"Are you, poor baby!" and conscious only of the sympathy the sweet face expressed, Diana stooped and kissed it involuntarily.

As if the touch of a woman's lips, the caress of a woman's hand was what he wanted, the boy rubbed his soft cheek against that softer one and nestled to her with a little sigh of pleasure, evidently hungry for the fostering tenderness mothers alone can give.

"I thought you were Aunt Alice and I want to see her, much, oh, very much," he said, stroking her hand and wrapping the folds of her dress about him like an unfledged bird anxious to be hidden under a sheltering wing.

"I wish I were. But I am very glad you came to me. I want a little friend and we can comfort one another," began Diana, full of interest in the small stranger and feeling as if she owed him some atonement for the disappointment.

But the kiss seemed to have satisfied him for the moment, sentiment gave place to curiosity and, taking advantage of the offer with childish promptitude, he released himself and beat upon the wall saying imperiously, "Lift me up. I wish to look over, Papa lets me."

Glad to keep her welcome playmate, Diana obeyed, and holding him fast, let him look abroad and shout to his heart's content, finding for herself a new pleasure in the mere touch of this chubby elf, so velvet soft, so full of life that thrilled her sensitive hands chilled by long contact with cold marble and damp clay. That innocent kiss had been like the stroke upon the clock and all the pent-up tenderness of her nature seemed to gush out, sprinkling the dust of what for a moment at least looked like a desert path along which she was following a mirage. She was amazed to feel how thirstily she drank of the sweet water so unexpectedly brought to her dry lips and laughed at herself even while she prolonged the drought, "for the child's sake," she thought.

"Dear little thing I must hold you fast or you will fly away as suddenly as you came," she said, wrapping him close in both arms as he danced upon the wall and flapped his arms with all the bright hair blowing in the wind.

He turned about to answer seriously, while he peeped under her hat brim and stroked her cheeks with innocent freedom. "I cannot fly. I like to stay, for you hold me nicely; Nanna shakes me so I run away. Papa's face is rough but yours is soft like Aunt Alice and so I love to kiss you," which he did impetuously, hugging close the new friend whose face and figure recalled the only mother he had ever known.

"I am glad of that. Now tell me your little name. I think it must be Angelino," said Diana, receiving with an almost shy delight the embraces of this small lover.

"It is an ugly name, but Papa makes it pretty. He calls me Nino. Do you like Antony Stafford more than that?" asked the boy with a grimace as if the rough name hurt his rosy little mouth.

"Yes, then Papa is a sculptor?" cried Diana quickly, for with the utterance of that name her eyes shone, and a hope sprung up in her heart that these childish hands might open a door before which she had often stood, longing yet not daring to knock.

"Oh yes, he makes marble things but I do not care for them. I like the nice, soft clay and I make birds and lambs, and once I made a lion!" said the boy, trying to mold his own blooming face into an expression of leonine ferocity.

The rolling eyes and puffed out cheeks were so droll that Diana laughed as she had not done for months, and the child laughed also with a gleeful prance.

"The lambs are best for such small fingers. I too work in the nice clay, and I shall love to make this face full of dimples if I can. Would not you like to see it in pretty white marble by and by, that will never break nor grow old?"

But Nino shook his head till all the curls flew wildly about, and sitting suddenly down he crossed the purple legs, took up the sketch book lying there and changed the subject by saying with immense decision, "No, I will not be pounded out of stone. It makes me ache to see the men do it. I will be only Nino and I will see these pictures. Tell me all about them."

Leaning beside him Diana obediently turned the pages best suited to his taste; telling where she saw the little goat that stood upon its hind legs to crop the grass among the crevices of the ruins; and how the boyish St. John was a bigger lad who stood as a model, and being cold with nothing on but his sheepskin, wrapped it round him and danced about the studio as one saw him there, a very jolly saint indeed. Coming to a priest Nino looked up to say, as he pointed with a chubby finger toward a procession of students winding like a scarlet thread along the paths below.

"Those are little ones, and when they grow up they will all wear black. Papa calls them lobsters." But just in the act of going off into another fit of merriment Nino saw his nurse approaching with anger in her black eyes, and a threatening gesture of a brown forefinger.

"No! No. I will not go, Nanna," he cried rebelliously, and dropping from the wall fled as fast as the sturdy legs would go, carrying his prize with him.

Pausing only to beg the Signorina's pardon for the spoiled bambino, Nanna hastened after him, scolding as she went while Diana awaited the capture with some anxiety as to the fate of her sketch book, rich in the fugitive fancies and helpful hints of an artist's brain and eye. But she had something better now to engross her thoughts than daydreams or the vague melancholy born of solitude and springtime.

Stafford was a well-known sculptor whose fame was already made, whose maturity was already crowned with success, but whose life had been eclipsed at noonday by the darkness of a great sorrow which seemed to have paralyzed the cunning hand and chilled the ambitious spirit just when both were ready to achieve their best. Diana knew the story well, the short sad romance that many had mourned over both for the man's and the artist's sake. The youth of brave struggle, the well-earned reward of fame and fortune at forty, then in the mid-summer of his life the happy love without which no success is perfect. One year of bliss and then the lovely English wife died, leaving a child to be an innocent reminder of the dearer because lost so soon. In the first anguish of this bitter disappointment Stafford could not bear the sight of the poor baby and, leaving it to the care of the mother's sister, went away to bury himself for five years. The world waited for him patiently, touched by such faithful grief (but waited in vain). He worked no more; and though to mortal ear he uttered no complaint but hid the sorrow in (the proud privacy of) a sacred silence, this carelessness of fame, this abandonment of the beloved art proved how deep the wound had been, how useless the balm which has power to heal most sorrows in a man's life. The death of the child's tender guardian recalled Stafford to his duty, and seeing the lovely boy now grown so like the lost mother, seemed to reawaken the father's heart and to fill it with love both passionate and remorseful.

He took the little creature entirely to himself, and devoted his life to it with a tenderness as entire as his neglect had been, finding unexpected solace in the childish affection that clung to him, the innocent face

94

that recalled the sweet one turned to dust. For the boy's sake a spark of the old ambition kindled slowly under the ashes of a burnt-out despair, and in the springtime new hopes began to cast a faint glow over the barren features, as the rosy bloom budded on the bare boughs of the peach trees along the grey hill sides.

Back to Rome he came with the child in his arms, opened the long disused studio and villa and seemed to wait only for new inspiration to take form and bear fruit for the beloved boy. As yet he had begun nothing, and the wide circle of friends and admirers that welcomed him back with a satisfaction both proud and tender looked consciously to see the rich fancy and gifted hand at work. But Stafford seemed in no haste to feel fresh laurels on a head too early grey, and was content for a time at least to handle only the soft limbs of the little, living statue given him to mold into a man.

Diana was thinking of this with an interest which few persons would have had the power to inspire in her mind, for she had looked upon Stafford as the man who did most honor to her chosen profession, had longed to see him, and when she did so at last in the streets of Rome, had watched him eagerly, never daring to make herself known, though in him she felt that she might find the help and counsel she was too proud to ask.

She had never chanced to see the boy or had not observed him, for hers were eyes that looked straight forward above the level of the little heads of children. Now and then when wearied of that steady gaze into the golden mist of the future, or the upward glance into the still more golden and distant world of an artist's highest heaven, she was glad to rest her eyes on the green grass and smell the wholesome earth from which so much beauty grows. In such a moment this human crocus thrusting itself up sunny and bold from the snows of death and sorrow looked into her face and wooed her touch, seeming all the fairer, the more attractive for the pain and passion of the romance out of which it sprang.

"I wish he would come back," she said to herself, when many minutes passed and no *repentent* truant appeared. The book bore her name and she felt sure of its return in time, but had she seen what messenger was bringing it, she would not have stood so tranquilly dreaming in the sunset.

The touch of that rosy mouth seemed to have unsealed the closely folded lips and left a smile there; the eyes that looked down upon the children playing on the terraces below were full of a new expression, wistful yet tender, and in her whole figure was something womanly and winning, as if the last clasp of childish arms had warmed the fair statue into still fairer flesh and blood. Her attitude was full of the unconscious grace of harmonious proportions, and as she leaned there, a slender yet stately figure in pale grey with no touch of color but the knot of crimson carnations in her bosom and the evening glow full on the face, half folds of a veil shrouded in folds of silvery gauze, she was a more attractive object than any marble nymph among the shrubs behind her.

Stafford, approaching with the book in one hand, the little rebel in the other, saw and recognized this beautiful woman as one whom he had observed with a sculptor's pleasure, passing through the streets like a grey nun unfolded in her own sweet thoughts and high purposes as in a veil that shut out the admiration of man's eyes. He was glad to find that the "pretty lady" Nino spoke of was this attractive person whose name he had discovered from the book, which likewise showed her talent and betrayed that she was the artist of whom he had heard, for on one page was a colorful drawing of the Saul. He would gladly have lingered a little as he went, to study her before she was conscious of his presence and confused by it as most women were, eager to show the sympathy and admiration alike distasteful to him. But Nino had no scruples about disturbing her, and quite unabashed by the mild rebuke he had received, ran gaily forward, crying in a shrill small voice, "Here is Papa; please tell him all about St. John and the pretty goat as you did me."

With the delightful freedom of a tenderly cherished child unused to repulse, he threw his arms about Diana, sure that his request would be granted. A little startled by the sudden onset she looked up to see a grey uncovered head bending above the yellow one, and heard a man's voice saying quietly, "I have to ask pardon this imp's rudeness and restore his theft. I find it easy to forgive him since a glance at its pages shows me that I have found a comrade whom it is a pleasure to know, if I may ask the honor?"

What she answered Diana never knew, for she was absorbed in one of those swift comprehensive glances with which a trained eye seizes a look for the significance of the countenance it rests on. "A rugged face steeped in genius" as someone has described a greater man, were the words which would best have described Stafford just then. Hair and head still dark below but white above as if with a sudden snow fall; eyes that would have been melancholy but for the fire of a courage nobler than pride, and aquiline features bronzed by the ardor of (Egyptian) Spanish skies. Straight and tall, he reminded her of the stone pines yonder, stately yet somber, their strong trunks defying the storm yet green recesses full of a sad murmur, lifted high above the world as if the sigh that haunted them was too sacred to be heard below.

"Tell us what that one is? Papa looked at it longest and liked it best. I did not because the man seems in pain," broke in the boy, possessing himself of the book and eagerly showing the page that held the figure of Saul.

Feeling as if "the imp" were in truth a spirit of good who was serving her in the sweetest way, Diana glanced with new pride as well as doubt at her work, and in a few expressive words explained the sketch. "I have heard of it, and hoping to meet you at some friend's house, I have delayed asking permission to come and see this fine piece of work," said Stafford, with a growing sense of pleasure in looking at the face that neither blushed nor smiled, nor avoided his commanding eyes, but met them with a clear and candid look while an expression of heartfelt satisfaction shone in every feature. He liked too the frank simplicity of her manner, for in it was both the gentle (pride) reserve of a woman accustomed to admiration and the glad humility of a pupil saluting a much honored master.

"You need not have waited, sir, since your name is a passport to any studio; and it is I who ask a favor in asking you to see my work," she said, laying the book upon the wall as Nino skipped away to chase a bird.

"How long have you been about this? Such things take time and patience to reach perfection," asked Stafford, glancing from the strong sketch to the slender hands which had remained ungloved since they turned the pictured pages for the boy.

"Four years, it is not in marble yet."

He liked that brief answer unfollowed by any complaint, for it showed that the woman could not only work but wait, crowning power with patience;

and his own successful hand held back the fluttering leaves with new respect and interest as he asked further questions in a tone that made it both easy and delightful to reply. Each felt the charm of this propitious hour, and the conversation was soon as frank and fluent as a mutual interest made the strangers friends by the freemasonry of their craft. The music died away, the sunset pageant faded, and the crowd thinned fast, but still they leaned there talking rapidly, conscious at first that Nino played about them, then forgetting him till he startled both by creeping along the parapet unperceived till he reached and caught his father round the neck. An involuntary motion of the man's swung the boy over the wall and but for Diana's quick gesture and strong grasp the precious little body would have rolled down the steep bank to fall broken on the stones far below. In the act of lifting him to safety, Stafford snatched him from her hold and clasped him tightly as if the mere thought of such a loss bereft him of self control for a moment. But Nino caught his breath and cried out lustily as he bent back his head with cheeks reddened by the passionate caresses his father gave them.

"I am not hurt! Your face is rough! I love to kiss the signorina best. Let me go to her and I will be good."

"Go then, naughty child, and thank her for saving you from destruction. You make a woman of me with your reckless pranks."

Stafford pushed the boy toward Diana and half turned away as if ashamed of the emotion he had betrayed. But Nino got no kisses, for Diana, with the wisdom few mothers would have found it possible to show just then, took the engaging torment by the chin, saying in a tone of soft severity which must impress the spoilt child by its novelty.

"You may thank me by promising not to do that dangerous thing again. Then I shall love to call on my little friend, and trust you not to frighten your father any more."

Grateful for the diversion, Stafford watched the boy with a smile that covered his own emotion and reassured the culprit, who looked perplexed at the unexpected penance demanded of his Highness.

"Now then, little Nino, repent and receive absolution as soon as possible for we must go before the mist rises," said the father anxious to house the child and fearing new mischief was brewing in that busy brain.

There was, for Nino had no thought of submission, and with an audacious laugh he snatched the carnations from Diana's bosom and scampered away impenitent and unforgiven.

"We will settle the account at bedtime and he shall thank you later. I will not try to do so now, but hope the time may come when I can prove how much I owe you."

He took off his hat and offered his hand with a look and gesture which said infinitely more than the moved tone in which he spoke, then hastened after the boy, leaving Diana to follow slowly, feeling as if almost anything were possible now.

"When will he come?" she said to herself many times during the next few days with more of the artist's than the woman's impatience. She pined to learn his opinion of her statue, for if *he* praised it she would be satisfied. *She* knew its faults, she also knew its power, and felt that few women had dared, or if daring had succeeded in doing such bold work as this. Strength had been her aim, not sentiment nor beauty. (These women can and have expressed in many shapes with varying success.) But power in visible form and undeniable truth is rare from men's hands, almost unknown from women's, and she thirsted to hear from lips whose praise was success the three words, "It is good."

The masculine fibre in her nature demanded recognition as it does in all strong natures, and having won it she could permit the softer side of her character to assert itself without fearing the accusation of weakness, which she hated like a man.

Eagerly she set her studio in order, brushed off the dust that had laid undisturbed so long upon her statue, and spent several of her carefully hoarded dollars for deep red drapery to hang behind it, feeling acutely how inadequate the dead plaster was to express what only marble could fitly embody and transfigure. Flowers she set about in graceful vases, and brought out a small store of art treasures to embellish the bare walls. She had never cared before, but now an honored guest was coming and she longed to make her domain beautiful not for her own sake but for that of the work it held.

Day after day went by, however, and still the desired guest did not come. But Diana had learned patience in a hard school and while she waited, fell to modelling a head of Nino, more because she found it impossible to settle to any other task than because she hoped for any great success. The pretty boy had brought her good fortune and a certain sense of gratitude seemed to constrain her to celebrate the event by an enduring memorial of the Puck whose spiriting had already done so much for her.

A week passed and Diana began to think with the sad resignation taught by many disappointments, "He will not come. He has forgotten like all the rest." On the seventh day she covered up the little head, wetting the damp cloth with a few quiet tears as if a hope as beautiful and innocent was dying fast, and went out into the garden to gather flowers for the vases seven times filled in vain.

Sitting on the fallen pillar by the fountain, she fell to dreaming with her lap full of trailing greenery and hands that forgot to tie up the last of her snowdrops and violets. So absent were her thoughts that she heard nothing till the sound of little feet on the path recalled her, and she looked up to see Nino dancing toward her with a great bunch of purple and yellow crocuses and anemones, crying as he came:

"*Buon giorno, signorina*! I gathered these all for you myself in the Pamphili Donia gardens, and Papa sent me to ask if he may come in."

Dispatching her permission by Maniuccia, who followed to announce *"Sua Eccelellenza,"* Diana paused a moment to welcome the child who breathlessly explained that he had been ill, and wanted to see her very much, but Papa would not go for her. Now he had come to see her himself, and where were the lizards she told him about?

When Stafford entered the studio he saw nothing but the pretty group framed by the open door that led into the garden; for to his eyes it was more beautiful than any other in all Rome. Nino was holding Diana fast, pleading with her to stay and tickle the lizards as she promised; and she was trying to escape with gentle eagerness. They looked like a mother and child at play, for the boy had caught her in a loop of ivy; she was caressing the small hands as she tried to force herself from their hold, and in the struggle the great nosegay had fallen apart deluging the pair with flowers. Both laughed, both golden heads were close together, and both faces were full of an innocent gaiety that made them lovely. Diana's cheeks were almost as rosy as Nino's, and her eyes shone and she was so happy that the long desired moment had come at last she willingly delayed that other meeting for a moment.

A pigeon alighting on the fountain's brim to drink attracted the boy and freed the captive who hastened in to find her guest examining the rough sketches on the walls, from which he turned with such an expression of almost tender interest that she involuntarily glanced at the familiar scrawls to see what caused it (he greeted her cordially).

"I sent Nino to explain the reason of our delay and make his peace. I was as impatient as he, so let me see at once. I have not even stolen a look, though much tempted."

With no answer but a grateful smile, Diana went straight to the curtain which hid her work and pushing it aside waited for the verdict. Stafford lifted his brows and stepped back a little as if surprised at the size of the statue. Then he stood looking silently, and as his eyes dwelt on it, they kindled, first with interest, then pleasure, then the satisfaction a master takes in recognizing excellence; and presently with a sudden illumination of the whole face he said slowly—"I am glad a woman did that."

"Because it's so weak?" Diana held her breath to hear the answer, doubting what she saw.

"Because it is so strong! There is virile force in this, accuracy as well as passion—in short, genius."

"Few men would say that to a woman." And Diana's voice shook with the irrepressible emotion which showed how intense her own anxiety had been, how exquisite was her joy at such commendation.

"Few women give us the chance to say it. We have had sentiment enough. Power conquers the proudest, and wrings the truth from the meanest. This is noble work, let me study it."

There was a pleasant sort of roughness in Stafford's manner, and he turned his back to look again. Diana liked this infinitely better than if he had overwhelmed her with compliments. It suited her to be forgotten in her work, and she stood mutely watching him as he walked about the statue, talking more to himself than to her, saying things that humbled by their sincere approval, and made her proud by their just criticism. This was what she wanted, and coming as it did was of immense value since the honest opinion of such a man was more to her than any medal she might hereafter win.

Presently he seemed to remember her, and turning, looked at her with the piercing glance which nothing appeared to escape. Keen but kind, and in it she saw a new respect dearer to her than any other homage. She bore the long gaze tranquilly, meeting it eye to eye with a fine mixture of honest pride and satisfaction in her own, such as a pupil might show a master over a hard lesson faithfully learned and justly praised. It seemed a fresh surprise and pleasure to find this sturdy sort of spirit in such a shape, and a sudden smile warmed his austere face as he offered his hand, giving hers the cordial grasp one man gives another when he says heartily, "Comrade, well done!"

"This must be hidden here no longer, but put in marble at once. Can you let it go?"

"I can; but ought I?" answered Diana quickly, feeling as if all her long cherished dreams were becoming beautiful realities at last. Her face showed her desire but the woman's dignity checked the artist's ardor, and she added slowly, "I have longed to see it done for years, yet I am slow to receive so great a favor even from so generous a hand."

"But not to grant one? Let me pay the debt I owe you and save your child from oblivion as you saved mine from harm. Obligation burdens me also, and I claim the right to fulfill the desire of your life, as you preserved the treasure of mine. So we are quits. You will consent?"

Asked in that way, how could she refuse? With most men she would have shrunk from such a service, but here she seemed to have earned it, for he not only thanked her as a woman but greeted her as an artist worthy of the name. The sculptor's satisfaction in her work was more to her than the father's gratitude, for such recognition was very precious to her sensitive pride, her love of justice, and the independence she cherished as she did her life. Her face grew soft and bright with confidence and happiness as she looked up after that instant's hesitation, yet there were tears in the eyes that were more eloquent than her few words.

"I do consent, and I thank you from my heart."

"It is I who am to be grateful; I who am glad to be the instrument which puts this fine creature before the world; I who will find the task a godsend. It shall be put in hand at once. My atelier is empty, my men wait for employment; I will give it to them, and when I hear the old music of the mallets I may find inspiration as well as occupation."

"Do you ever need it?" Diana asked involuntarily, struck by the air of mingled desire and despondency with which he spoke.

"Always, *now* for the power has gone out of me. My friend, may you never know the awful weariness that comes when the golden apples one has struggled for turn to ashes on the lips."

The words seemed to break from him against his will, and were so full of bitter sadness, while over the strong face there swept such a tragic shadow that for one instant Diana felt as if her Saul had spoken.

A woman's instinct prompted the happy answer to that involuntary betrayal of the disappointment which but for one tie would have deepened to a fixed despair.

"You have the boy to live and work for. Is not that an aim and a consolation?" she asked, with a gentle frankness that made its undertone of sympathy the sweeter.

"It shall be! Pardon the complaint; it was wrung from me by the memory of the time when I saw *my* first success and rejoiced in it as you do now. I thought the cup was full then, but one bitter drop turned the wine to wormwood, and I have not learned yet to drink it patiently."

The room was very still for a moment, and nothing broke the silence but the soft babble of the fountain and the boy's voice cooing with the doves. As if the music of this little David soothed the troubled soul of the man, Stafford turned to the sunny doorway and stood there asking himself why this woman unconsciously allowed such confidence from him, unless it was that in her he saw curiously blended an image of his own ambitious youth and a faint likeness to the wife he mourned.

Full of pity and anxious to divert his thoughts, Diana dropped the curtain before her great work with one glance of exultation, and busied herself in unwrapping the little head of Nino, sure that only pleasant fancies could be stirred by the pretty thing.

"See what I have dared to do without permission. He is so beautiful I could not resist the desire to keep him. I am often tired of attempting [fraud impossibilities] and find repose and delight in work like this."

"That is charming! My very Nino, imp and angel all in one. Lift the hair just here, and curl the corners of the (lips) mouth here. He has his mother's perfect lips, poor baby!"

If Diana had sought for comfort suited to his mood, she could have found nothing better than this, for both man and sculptor felt the tender tact with which she touched the one happy note that made music for him, and he thanked her for it by the air of relief and pleasure he wore as he watched her at work. It was as if he saw a woman giving the motherless boy the gentle caress he needed, for she used no tool, but with her own deft fingers twined the little curls back from the brow, caressed the soft contour of the cheek in smoothing it, and moulded the pouting lips to Nino's own naughty smile as if remembering the kisses they had given her unasked.

"That is my bambino, and I am truly glad you did it. I have often begun but could never finish, yet I should have done it, these frail little lives are so easily blown out," he said, making one effective dent in the round chin which gave Nino's dimple to the life and he smiled as if his fingers felt the charm of their old mastery as they hovered above the small ear, and touched the fine arch of the baby head.

"I shall take great satisfaction in finishing it for you sir, if I may," said Diana, infinitely gratified to have found a way to lighten, even a little, the favor which she knew could oppress her in spite of the grace of its bestowing.

"I shall accept it with sincere delight. It pleases me to find that the hand which grappled so bravely with the difficulties of that Saul can also put such tender truth into a baby's face. I bereave you of your giant but I will lend you the pretty pigmy as often as you like in return."

As if to make good his father's promise, Nino appeared at the moment, announcing that he was hungry. Gladly Diana brought forth her little store of sugar biscuits and dates hanging like great amber drops from the stem they grew upon, and fed the child, who leaned against her knee, contentedly smearing his lip with honey and scattering crumbs over the purple lap that held his plate. Stafford meantime was roving about the studio, apparently seeing only evidences of hopeful work everywhere and commending it heartily; yet in reality reading the story of the woman's life in that solitary room, and admiring her genius the more for the hard soil out of which the rare flower had sprung.

Entirely forgetful of herself, Diana talked eagerly and well on the topics most dear to her, inspired to do so by the cordial interest her guest expressed, and the rich experience out of which he spoke. To him there was something piquant in listening to the boldest of opinion from this handsome creature's lips, uttered with a certain calm conviction and unsparing truthfulness which contrasted curiously with the patient care with which she put one sweet morsel after another into the rosy mouth held up so persistently, and the tender zeal with which she washed a pair of dirty little hands after the feast was over.

"One feels as if there was a fine man and a fine woman working *there* together, and one scarcely knows which to admire most," he thought to himself as he went away, leaving Diana to work with enthusiasm on the arched head of the boy, to which she added a pair of winged shoulders and called it Puck.

CHAPTER IV

At Home

"Now I will go and see how well Percy's experiment succeeds. If she can combine art and domestic life harmoniously she will be a more remarkable woman than even I think her."

This resolved Diana on receiving the happy letter which told of the birth of Percy's little daughter in the early spring. She had been longing to go to her friend with a desire which sometimes was almost irresistible; but a certain proud yet sad conviction that she was no longer first and dearest restrained her till these last letters, full of such blissful content, such loving entreaties to come and see and rejoice over the one perfect and delicious baby in the world, proved too strong for her and she answered promptly.

"I will come, deluded dear, as soon as I can set my affairs in order and store away my children, for fortunately I am not a slave to them as you are to (that impertinent baby of yours) your latest work."

But even her marble offspring proved somewhat difficult to dispose of; and her small affairs took some time to settle, so it was several months before Diana sailed. She did not warn Percy of her approach but promised herself the pleasure of taking her by surprise, and discovering if this happy family was in truth all her friend's glowing pen had painted it.

Arriving at Paris in the evening, Diana was glad to go with some pleasant fellow travellers to a hotel for the night. Bewildered and excited by the novelty of all she saw and heard, she felt like one released from the quiet solitude of a prison cell and suddenly turned loose into the big, bustling world. Few guessed the inward perturbation, however, for her natural dignity and self control seemed undisturbed and stood her in good stead now.

Next morning she set bravely forth alone to find her friend, for by no word or message would she spoil the long contemplated surprise with which she hoped with a woman's tender sort of malice to avenge the years Percy had been happy without her. The gay city looked its best in the brilliant June weather, and as Diana glided away by sail to one of its most beautiful environs through blooming gardens and orchards, she felt as if passing out of the small, dull world of reality into the enchanting regions of romance, and gave herself up to the new charm with the wondering delight of a child turning for the first time the pages of a fairy story.

Holding Percy's description as a clue, she easily found her way to the little villa on the hillside, but even while her heart beat fast with the joy of the expected meeting, she was constrained to pause in the gateway and look about her at the lovely view which makes that spot famous. Down the terraced slope to the wide river winding down under the airy viaduct, through the green valley, up the opposite bank, and away over the billowy, blooming landscape swept the delighted eye to where afar off in a golden haze the great city shone against the landless azure of the sky. Spring fragrance filled the balmy air from the little garden behind her, white curtains fluttered from the windows above as if to welcome her, and like the sound of a brooding wood dove came a familiar voice, with a new tone of tenderness in it, cooing a lullaby in the room that opened on the balcony.

Holding her breath to enjoy this delicious moment (waited for so long) to the uttermost, Diana looked up with eager eyes, hoping to catch a glimpse of the dear face, but saw only a man's dark head bent as if over a book, and [as] she turned to enter, the notes of a violin arrested her, so exquisitely fine and clear was the strain, so in keeping with the fair scene, the happy hour, the softened mood that filled her eyes with sudden tears and set wide the doors of her heart to let a new emotion in.

As the music ended, a voice cried "Now August, do put down the violin and let me have my way with you while I can." Percy's voice, and as if the sound drew her straightway in, Diana hastened up the white steps, through doors standing wide as if to let in the spring, to the threshold of a room which seemed familiar, she had so often studied the sketch of Percy's little home. A little home it looked indeed, as the newcomer took it all in with one comprehensive glance, for Percy's husband sat in the antique chair, his violin dropped to his knee, smiling with the silent satisfaction of a man whose eyes behold the treasures of his life; Percy's baby lay like a pink and white apple blossom blown in upon the Persian rug that half covered the polished floor, a tiny, three months creature, but full of life as it lay cooing in the sunshine with the soft, aimless motion that says so much to women's eyes; and Percy herself sat low beside her little daughter, busily sketching the face she loved best in all the world.

Diana had time to see no more, for as her eye touched her friend she looked up, uttered a glad cry, and flew to meet her in the old impulsive way.

"My dearest girl! All this long journey alone and never let me know! August, it is Di, really come to us at last."

Down went violin and bow as quickly as drawing board and crayon and up rose Percy's husband to greet her friend with almost equal cordiality though fewer words.

"You are most welcome! Now Percy will be quite content."

"Indeed I shall, for now I have all I love safe in my own home. See, dear, this is August and this my little Di, the champion baby of the world."

She might more truly have been called the best baby for she certainly was a good baby, for she bore her mother's rapturous snatching with a great nerve, uttering no protest except a hiccough as she was held proudly forth to be admired, winking at her godmamma like a little owl.

"A dear baby, Heaven bless her!" and Diana was surprised at the warmth with which she kissed and embraced her small namesake, for children did not usually interest her.

"Now take her, Papa, while I make Di comfortable and show her all my kingdom, it won't take long," and with a blithe laugh Percy tucked the baby into the capacious cradle of her father's arms where she evidently felt as much at home as the violin.

"Here is my studio; just one peep and then leave it for by and by," continued Percy, showing a second salon which, judging from the dust upon the easel and the dried up paint upon the palette, had not been very lately used.

Diana's quick eye saw it and Percy read the meaning in her look, but ignored it except by the haste with which she dropped the portière and hastened to open a door across the passage, saying as she flung wide the door, "This is the blue room especially prepared for you. Sly creature, if you had only let me know when you were coming it would have been less stuffy. Never mind, you are come and that is joy enough. Dear Di, you look so pale now, I'm afraid you have been pining for me, selfish woman that I am." exclaimed Percy, holding her close and then falling back to study her face with remorseful solicitude.

"I wanted you, but you were happy so I did not pine. I am only a little tired with my journey. Now I am safely here I shall soon be as rosy and gay as yourself. How well and glad and beautiful you look, my Percy," answered Diana, examining in turn with admiring surprise.

In truth she did look so, for the first happy year of married life that blesses many women had been an unusually serene and perfect one to Percy and its tender glow still beautified her face, as the morning red transfigures all things for one fresh and dewy hour. Not only was she lovelier but more noble, for she had passed through the deep experience which sanctifies forever in heart and memory the coming of the first born. The touch of those baby hands had not only baptized her with a holy happiness but laid upon her sacred responsibilities, endless duties, higher aspirations, and she accepted them devoutly. But something of the youthful audacity was gone, and the eyes that had looked so fearlessly into the future for herself began to wear the tender anxiety that mother's eyes take on when peering hopefully, prayerfully into the unknown future of a child. This was a fleeting expression however, only seen at thoughtful moments on a face full of the supreme content, the happy energy of a woman living her most precious hours and eager to lose no instant of their sunshine.

"Now tell me all about your plans, for if I once begin my gossip I warn you it is a story without an end," said Percy, hovering about her guest, to put by hat and mantle, and do the honors of the muslin-draped toilet table, and with her own affectionate hands smooth the pale gold braids that always crowned the stately head. "Come then and sit together on this pretty lounge in the window, so that I can feast my eyes on that enchanting view. It held me fast outside and I cannot keep away from it even now," said Diana, drawing her hostess down beside her, forgetting her story for a moment as she leaned to look again into the green abyss before her, to glance up at the ruined chateau above or let her eyes wander to the shining domes and spires in the distance.

"If that were not wicked Paris I should say it looked like the Celestial City in this light," she added enthusiastically, yielding herself to the spell which draws so many to this woman city of the world.

"It has been almost that to me," answered Percy, with sweet seriousness. "One can find Heaven anywhere when one loves and is beloved. Oh, Di, it has been such a rich and perfect year. I never knew how much a human being can enjoy, and only wonder how I ever lived so long alone," she added fervently.

"Early days yet, Percy; enjoy while you may but don't expect it to be midsummer always," Diana regarded her with the affectionate compassion which the uninitiated usually show for those whom love's glamour blinds to the possibility of there ever being a rough side to life.

"I knew you'd say that, and take immense comfort in pitying my delusion. I'm ready to be scolded, and won't try to defend myself if you will only like August and admire the baby," said Percy, smiling down upon her from the serene heights of her indescribable and seemingly unassailable repose.

"I take them both on trust and promise to admire; especially the baby. I have often wanted one to model and now if you will let me I should like to try it while you paint your lord and master. Do you know, Percy, that to find you hard at work was an inexpressible comfort to me," and Diana's tone of intense satisfaction betrayed how her fear had been that these new obstacles would have proved fatal to all progress.

Percy laughed in her sleeve, for half an hour earlier Diana would have found (caught) her with a dust cap on, sweeping her little parlor while August rocked the baby and Fanchette scolded about the marketing. Her eyes twinkled mirthfully but she divulged no domestic secrets and answered with an air of demure conviction. "Then we could not have posed better if we had studied to please you? I am glad of that, for really, Di, I want you to see and acknowledge that it is possible to put my theory in practice. I have done a good deal of work this last year — how could I help it with August to inspire and criticize and rejoice over me. Even Baby is not much of an interruption, she is such a little angel. Papa says her artistic tastes are already developing. I really think she notices colors and I know he can always quiet her with music."

"Then the angel does occasionally cry?" said Diana, with a provoking readiness to spy out a thorn upon the rose.

"My dear, she is a mortal child and must have her little ailments; though why the innocent would be so plagued with wind I cannot see. August jokes about it in the most unfeeling way, and says she shall play the flute when he is first violin, she can hold her breath so long in a crying yell," and Percy's face was a droll muscle of maternal piety and girlish fun, as she recalled some of the musical nights the family had spent together.

Diana looked a little scandalized, but seemed to enjoy watching her friend in this new role, very much as the chaste goddess might have looked down upon some shepherd's happy wife before she found her own Endymion and kissed him in his sleep.

"You always did love your dolls, and were never happier than when all six were dangerously ill, I remember. Your experience will be of use to you now, I'm sure," she said, with her soft, sarcastic smile as she glanced at a tiny bottle labelled "Chamomilla" thrust into one of Percy's buttonholes as if ready for emergencies.

"I think it is, seriously, Di, for I am learning to manage my baby nicely and she is a healthy creature, thank heaven. Among the books you sent me from home was an old one of Grandma's, 'A Young Mother's Friend,' full of receipts, directions, and notes in her own hand, and it has been such a help to me. Dear Grandma! Though she is gone her loving care still seems to follow and surround me. How I wish I could lay my baby on her lap where my mother left her little baby girl and both of us be folded in her arms together once."

A few bright drops fell from Percy's eyes in memory of her loss, proving that the new love had not dimmed the old, although its balm had taken all the bitterness from sorrow. The beloved name was a key to unlock the hearts of both, and for an hour they sat together giving and receiving with tears and tender talk the sacred legacy of those last peaceful words and days, forgetting present joy to live again the grief that drew them closer and bridged across the years of absence. They were just passing on to Diana's plans when a little impatient cry, which had been smothered more than once, burst out imperiously and arrested further confidences, for at the sound Percy sprang up, saying as she hurried away full of maternal compunction, "I must go to Baby! Rest and refresh yourself, Di, then come to us and have lunch; I won't insult your Puritan ears by calling it *déjeuner.*"

Stretching herself upon the couch, Diana nested luxuriously, examining the pretty chamber as she lay, and listening to the sounds from the adjoining room which interested, amused and enlightened her.

"Poor little girl! was she neglected by her bad, forgetful mother? Come now and go to byelow in her own nest like a drowsy darling as she is." And Percy's voice began again the pretty German Sleep Song as contented murmurs from young Di expressed her pardon.

But the lullaby was frequently interrupted by directions and remarks in a sing-song tone that neither lunch nor deluded Baby's nap might be retarded.

"Papa, dear, would you just step into the garden and get a handful of flowers for the table? I was so busy this morning that I had not time, and I want things to be nice for Di As you go out, please tell Fanchette to be very careful about the salad dressing, and since you have your hat on, you might run around the corner and get fresh oil—yes and some strawberries, they are so effective whether sweet or sour. Only, dearest man, don't, I beg of you, march in and give your bundles to me before company, as you did when the fine Hammonds were here. I don't mind Di so much, but you must be trained, my love. How do you like her: a handsome creature, isn't she?"

"Doubtless, but I have scarcely seen her, she was swept away so soon," answered the man's voice, deep and strong above the low chant of the woman.

"You will like her, I am sure of it, because she is your sort, silent, brave and self reliant; proud too and with a will of her own. Ah, you may regret that you did not see her before you wasted yourself on a poor thing like me," said Percy, (with) in a stifled tone suggestive of a little hand held against her lips.

"No fear, the same unlikeness which makes her thy friend makes *me* thy happy husband. Shall I order a sweet dish at the *pâtissier*'s when I get the fruit? We must do honor to this guest of ours."

"We will save that for Sunday. Fanchette will make an omelette-soufflé, and with coffee it will be enough. There, Baby is off already, little dear! While I go to lay her down, will you pull out the big portfolio and the heads from the high shelf. Di was pleased to find me at work and I never told her what a lazy woman I have been lately."

"Lazy! I often think I let thee do too much, my busy little housemother."

Here Diana felt herself in honor bound to cough aloud that her hosts might be reminded of her proximity, though by so doing she deprived herself of any further domestic revelations. Steps departed, doors closed, and silence reigned, but Diana could not resist peeping from behind the blue curtains for a glimpse of this unknown August who had usurped her place in Percy's life. She had been too shy to look at him before, except one glance as he took her hand, receiving only an impression that he *was* a little like the pictures she had seen of Shelley. A tall, slender gentleman moving about the little garden, careless alike of the wind that blew his hair into his eyes or the thorns that pricked his fingers as he hastily pulled roses from the trellis and threw them into his hat, looking as if the oil and strawberries, sketches and salad dressing laid a little heavy on his mind and memory. A fine head it seemed, with clustering dark hair, and a face full of that indescribable something which is better than beauty in a man, a certain nobility of expression, the sure index of a character in which rectitude and resolution reign. With an artist's eye Diana scorned the outward semblance of the man, with a friend's solicitude she tried to guess the inward nature, and with a woman's quick yet inexplicable instinct she felt that she should like him, rival though he was.

Just as this feeling came to her and she involuntarily leaned out from her ambush to see him pass below, he looked up suddenly, smiled, bowed and paused to say, with a swift comprehension of the thought in her face, which would have been rather startling but for the playfulness of the question — "Well, mademoiselle, am I to be forgiven?"

"For what?" asked Diana, coloring with surprise yet looking down with a glance almost as steadfast as that which met her own in what she now saw were "the blue and constant eyes of the North."

"For robbing you of Percy, I know what it is; I too have had friends taken from me and found it so hard to bear that I was tempted to console myself in like manner."

"Since she is happy I forgive you," answered Diana, smiling back at him, for the look said far more than the words and touched a sympathetic chord in her lovely heart.

"You are magnanimous. In her name I thank you and reward you." And he threw up a great red rose which lit on Diana's breast and seemed to warm the cool grey of her dress as pleasantly as these new interests gave color to her life.

She nodded and set the flower in her buttonhole, feeling that the ice was broken by the little compact between them, then watched August as he came out again and went away to do his errands with a good will that lent romance even to prosaic marketing.

Curious to see Percy at work, she went presently, to look for her, but stopped on the way to examine the studies set forth in the pretty little salon. These absorbed her while Percy came in to lay the table, giving glimpses of a tiny kitchen where a white-capped *bonne* was beating eggs with vigor, for they only occupied an apartment in the villa and kept but a single maid. The dining room had been sacrificed to the studio, and the salon did double duty, so art gossip and table setting went on harmoniously together, though the cream pot was inadvertently upset into the stream of chat, and Fanchette did not achieve a perfect omelette, being distracted by her efforts to observe the distinguished stranger through the keyhole.

August soon returned; but discreetly shut himself into a pantry which with difficulty held him while he concealed the guilty parcels and then strolled into the parlor with the satisfied expression of a man who has executed a delicate maneuver with skill and been rewarded for it. Diana enjoyed the innocent little farce immensely, and was found smiling in the face of a grim Medusa when her host came to do the honors of the big portfolio, while her hostess set forth her small store of silver, glass and china in festival array, proudly brought in salad and fruit, hot coffee and cold chicken with delectable rolls and a pot of butter still in its grape leaf fresh from the dairy, saying gaily as she placed flowers in the midst—"Now if I could serve Baby among the roses my feast would be complete. As I cannot, admire if you please my fine jar of old Delft, and let August fill your glass with the wine we keep for red letter days like this."

So they ate and drank gaily together, with all the loveliness of spring outside, and the greater loveliness of love itself inside, touching everything with its peculiar charm. The sense of having stepped into a romance grew upon Diana momentarily, and she kept saying to herself, "I shall wake presently in the old studio at home." But she had no wish to wake, for she heartily enjoyed this glimpse of the sweet old story forever being told the wide world over, and forever full of enchantment for those who read as for those who write it.

Percy talked most and with all her accustomed enthusiasm, whether it was of Rome or railroads, ancient history or modern baby blankets, and into everything she said and did, she put such fun and fancy that the little salon rang with innocent merriment and Fanchette smiled involuntarily among her casseroles in the kitchen. August did his share with spirit and skill, proving himself to Diana's delight an art lover and art critic of no mean order. With feminine tact the women ignored a past in which he had no part and discussed topics of general interest; but allusions and reminiscences, old hopes and projects insensibly slipped into their conversation, enlightening him as to many things he had never known or vaguely guessed before. Presently he fell silent and sat watching Percy while she listened to Diana's plans with a growing ardor in her face, an unconscious tone of regret now and then in her eager voice, an entire absorption in the subject which for the first time in her married life made her forgetful of his presence. His eye went from one face to the other, resting longest upon Diana's which he scrutinized with intense but covert interest as if trying to read the character of this friend whose influence he already saw was much stronger than he had imagined.

No jealousy mingled with the very natural anxiety which grew upon him, lest the new element should disturb the peace of home, very precious to a man so long homeless. The generous desire that Percy should have all the happiness life could give her, even if he were not the donor, struggled with a fear that, by this rousing (of) the old ambitions, something of the old unrest and discontent might mar the beautiful repose which had possessed her for a year. He knew by sad experience how hard the effort is to bind a passionate desire and hold it captive at the feet of duty, yet he also knew what rich compensations such sacrifices sometimes bring, since mastery of oneself is nobler than mastery of the world. He was more ambitious for this young wife of his, both as woman and artist, than she was herself, but man-like he loved the woman best, and yearned to keep her for a little longer all his own. Time enough for glory by and by, just now he did not want his Paradise invaded even by admiring angels, and a shadow crept into the eyes that watched Diana, as if she were the fair serpent who was beguiling his impetuous Eve to taste the ruddy apple she had nibbled at already.

He drank the last drops in his neglected coffee cup, finishing them both cold and bitter since Percy had forgotten to replenish it, and at the next pause in the lively conversation he rose, saying with gay and friendly air which seemed native to him, "My half holyday has been so unexpectedly celebrated that I am tempted to make a whole one of it. I will leave you to your coffee gossip while I go to town for an hour or two and be back again by the time your projected works rival those of Raphael and Michael Angelo."

"Yes, dear, and don't forget to see that Di's luggage comes out safely. I gave you the list of things for Baby this morning. Oh, and get, please, a canvas 18 by 20, I shall go to work at once upon your portrait in oils. And don't be late, August, because we must show Di the old chateau at sunset," added Percy, holding her husband by both lapels of his coat to impress her directions upon his mind.

"My friend, I shall remember."

"He really will, for he is one of the few men who have a memory for women's commissions," said

Percy, looking around with a face full of wifely pride in this unusual accomplishment.

"One woman's commissions, would be a closer statement, Madame," began August with masculine accuracy, but Percy stopped him with a kiss, and he departed, only saying with a grave sort of tenderness, which Diana liked better than any gush of sentiment, "Do not tire thyself, else thee can not walk at sunset."

He made the "hour or two" as long as possible, yet when he returned they were still hard at it. He found them in the studio where there had evidently been a great resurrection of the past two or three years' work, for there was a mild confusion of studies and sketches, panels and portraits in every sort of style. He also found them both drawing from the nude, their model being his cherished daughter set forth in the costume of a Cupid on a red cushion in the sunshine, where she lay decidedly enjoying her little self, for the pink legs, freed from petticoats, kicked delightedly and a pair of dimpled arms moved like wings making ready for a flight.

Both women were intent upon this task, working as rapidly as they talked, with frequent bursts of laughter at the impossibility of catching the pretty poses of their lively model. There was a brilliant color in Percy's cheeks, her eyes shone with unusual fire, and she wore what her husband called her painting frenzy look, an excited, absorbed expression which he had not seen since she used to come in after a successful day at the Gallery in London. The shadow flittered across his face again, but was gone in a moment as he joined involuntarily in their merriment when Baby, staring vaguely at nothing, hit her own minute nose with a soft fist and gasped like a little gold fish with surprise at the exploit.

"Unnatural mother! Would you sacrifice your child on the altar of your insatiable art?" he demanded, pointing tragically at the placid squirmer as he joined them.

Diana looked rather conscience-stricken, for she had proposed the immolation; but Percy promptly whipped Baby into her blue blanket—as she said, nothing daunted—"She always has a sun bath and can't take cold for the windows are all shut. But we must wait, Di, till she is asleep; one might as well try to draw an eel awake. Kiss your stern father, child, and tell him you are to be immortalized in marble by and by."

She held up the blue bundle with such loving pride and looked so happy that August gladly listened and agreed to all she told him, promising to order clay tomorrow and expressing great interest in the work but wisely keeping to himself the opinion that no living artist could do justice to the exquisite little piece of sculpture in his arms.

Percy was very quiet through dinner and lest the evening walk should be spoilt, took her turn at listening while Diana and August talked. She was proud of her husband then, for he had read much and of the best; his English was excellent, and only an occasional phrase or accent betrayed him and when interested he talked fluently and well. Diana's reserve soon melted in this genial atmosphere, and she was insensibly won to do her best, proving that her seclusion had not been a narrow one, since high thoughts make a world for themselves, and a purposeful life enriches itself from every attainable source. So Percy listened well pleased, and left them still discussing Ruskin while she went to put Baby to bed, leaving Fanchette to guard the treasure while she was away.

As the lovely day waned toward its still lovelier close, the three set forth to watch the pageant of the western sky from the ruins of the old chateau. Diana looked with surprise at Percy who with garden hat upon her head, a piece of knitting in her gloveless hands, walked beside her husband, nodding to white-capped women and blue-bloused men, artists loitering home after a hard day's work, trying to paint the unpaintable, or families supping on their doorsteps in the social French fashion.

"Don't look shocked, dear piece of propriety; you will come to it in time and enjoy the freedom as I do. It is a charming way to live, so simple, friendly and picturesque. I never can go back to the old cumbersome dull fashion again," said Percy, strolling along with her fingers busily shaping a tiny sock while her eyes were revelling in the tender nuances of color fading from the sky.

"I was only wondering what some of our friends at home would say to see the elegant Miss Lennox now. I'm afraid they would not enjoy it as I do, for it suits you, excellently and I like it," answered Diana, pocketing her own gloves and yielding to the carefree influences all about her.

"We used to take our books and work and suffer and camp where we pleased, getting as hearty, brown and gay as these good neighbors of ours. As soon as my daughter is old enough, I shall pack her on my back like a gypsy mother, let her tumble on the wholesome grass while I sketch and Papa improves my mind."

"The pleasant times you used to tell of in your letters. You must not let me interrupt them. Everything is so new to me I cannot fail to enjoy whatever comes," said Diana, looking about her with wide eyes, and drawing in long breaths of the balmy air like a

125

thirsty traveller who has found the much desired spring at last.

"A summer here with us, if you do not tire of our quiet ways, will prepare you for the still greater freedom of artistic life in Italy," said M. Muller, quite unconscious that he added much to the picturesqueness of their group by wearing a slouch hat and carrying Percy's red shawl flung carelessly over a black velvet shoulder.

"Not a summer, thank you; I must have a glimpse of Switzerland before I cross the Alps, for I may never come back and must snatch all I can as I go. Some friends who I met in London invited me to join them in July and I could not deny myself the pleasure."

"Only a month? I will not hear of it, Di! Go to Switzerland for the hot season, I want you to see August's wonderful country, but come back to us in September, and let us start you safely off to Rome a month or two later," cried Percy, feeling as if this sight of her friend only made it the harder to give her up again.

"I promise if you want me; but I fear I may be an intruder in this happy little home of yours, for the honeymoon does not seem to be over yet," answered Diana, below her breath, as M. Muller lingered behind to gather some blossoming grasses by the wayside.

"Many people would be but not you," said honest Percy, adding with a backward glance, "I want you two to be friends. He will like you, I am sure, and you him if you wait a little, he does not wear his heart on his sleeve as I do, but oh, he is far better worth the knowing."

"We shall see. Do you ever regret the old life, Percy?"

"Never!" she uttered the word with such energy that her husband heard it and looked the question which he did not ask. Percy laughed at her own warmth and explained, taking his arm as if to make herself a tie between the two.

"It will be a very bitter hour to me when I discover that she finds her loss greater than her gain." M. Muller looked from under the wide hat brim with something like reproach in the eyes which were always a surprise to Diana, having in them nothing of the Southern fire and softness which would have matched his warm coloring and dark hair.

He directed his reply to her, and in it she fancied there lurked a warning or an appeal, and felt a little guilty that her question had been asked. Both were already conscious of the affectionate jealousy, the spirit of rivalry with which they could not help regarding the richly endowed woman who stood between them, since they represented the two strong passions which divided her heart and ruled her life.

"To me also, since the choice is so happily made. But you know the wiseacres say we women cannot have all, and must decide between love and fame, so I am curious to see which of us will fare the best," said Diana lightly, hoping to slip away from the dangerous subject with a jest.

But Muller answered with an earnestness which impressed her then and was remembered long afterward, as he laid his hand upon his wife's as if bestowing all he asked for her.

"Pardon, I believe a woman can and ought to have both if she has the power and courage to win them. A man expects them, achieves them, why is not a woman's life to be as full and free as his? The road may be different, but the end is the same and the prizes should be justly given. Love alone is not enough for any large and hungry soul, it should have all it can hold, else it has thwarted the purpose of its Maker."

Surprise kept Diana silent, but her face betrayed her and Percy exulted over her with delight.

"There, Di! Could the most liberal-minded American say more than that? I did not convert him, he came to it himself through his own love of liberty, being a free Switze with a great hatred for tyrants as our glorious William Tell himself."

"Yes, truly! I not only cherish this belief but I hope to see it beautifully realized by the success of this splendid wife of mine, who is to be the greater artist for being a happy woman, please God." And Muller lifted his hat as if registering a bow, with a flash of the eyes that showed he meant it.

Diana bowed gravely, charmed with his warmth but not one whit convinced by it, for her opinion on this point was as firmly fixed as Mont Blanc.

"You see, I have someone to fight my battles for me now, and I find it very comfortable. You and August can argue that vexed question as often and as fiercely as you like and I'll sit by enjoying it. Meantime I propose a truce while you admire the view." And Percy waved the little sock like a white flag before the contending parties as she led them to the platform whence one could look far and wide.

Diana enjoyed it vastly, and they sat there till twilight fell, and with it the dew. Then Muller wrapped Percy in her shawl and took her home with a gentle sort of authority which she seemed to like, while Di secretly resented it, preferring to wait for moonrise. As if she guessed her friend's mood, Percy, having obediently laid herself upon the sofa, proposed music, sure that such playing as August's would have charms to soothe a far more savage breast than dear old Di's.

Glad to be allowed to spend the evening in the way which best atoned to him for a day of absence and irksome duty, Muller gave them some exquisite things from Midsummer Night's Dream, with the fitting accompaniment of wondering wind, soft dusk and the rustle of leaves eager for the coming of the elves.

Diana, sitting beside the couch with Percy's hand often stealing into hers full of mute eloquence, listened thirstily, for the artistic temperament keenly enjoys all forms of beauty, and her ear drank in the music which fed her soul as did the loveliness on which her eye dwelt. Nor was it sensuous pleasure only, for finer influences were at work, and though no word was spoken, music and moonlight made the strangers friends.

As August played he seemed to make the little instrument speak for him, and its truthful tones expressed the man better than any picture painted even by the loving artist near him. The mingled strength and lightness of the touch, the sweet whispering notes, the sad undertones that crept in here and there, the thrilling chords, full of passionate pathos, the fine clear echo of the climbing harmony melted into silence with no fall to mar the strain that seemed to lift and leave the listener at Heaven's gate.

Diana felt all this, and found herself saying, "He is worthy of her, and will work the miracle if man can."

But while she listened with closed eyes, the moonlight stole into the room and shone upon her face, never more beautiful than now when hope and happiness were leading her across the hills she had climbed so patiently into the land of promise for such as she. Percy did not see it, for she was thinking what they should have for breakfast, since morning would inevitably bring that dreadful question. But August, playing on, looked out from his shadowy corner at the figure bathed in light, finding it not only fair but winning, for the keen eyes were shut now, the firm lips smiled, the proud head leaned like a drowsy flower, and the whole face was softened wonderfully, not only by the magic of the moon but by the unwonted mood which unlocked her heart, and for an hour showed how much unsuspected tenderness it held.

"She is not all the artist but a woman to be loved as well as admired. I will not be afraid, but trust her as Percy does," he said within himself, and as if relieved from some unacknowledged fear he passed suddenly from a melancholy Nocturne to such gay dance music that it startled both listeners wide awake, leaving Percy undecided between fish or cutlets, and Diana wondering if she could be happy with a musical husband in a home like this.

So they went merrily to bed, and the rivals shook hands with new cordiality as they said "Good Night!"